The Boxcar Children
Surprise Island
The Yellow House Mystery
Mystery Ranch
Mike's Mystery
Blue Bay Mystery
The Woodshed Mystery
The Lighthouse Mystery
Mountain Top Mystery
Schoolhouse Mystery
Caboose Mystery
Houseboat Mystery
Snowbound Mystery
Tree House Mystery
Bicycle Mystery
Mystery in the Sand
Mystery Behind the Wall
Bus Station Mystery
Benny Uncovers a Mystery
The Haunted Cabin Mystery
The Deserted Library Mystery
The Animal Shelter Mystery
The Old Motel Mystery
The Mystery of the Hidden
   Painting
The Amusement Park Mystery
The Mystery of the Mixed-Up Zoo
The Camp-Out Mystery
The Mystery Girl
The Mystery Cruise
The Disappearing Friend Myste
The Mystery of the Singing Gh
Mystery in the Snow
The Pizza Mystery
The Mystery Horse
The Mystery at the Dog Show
The Castle Mystery
The Mystery of the Lost Village
The Mystery on the Ice
The Mystery of the Purple Pool
The Ghost Ship Mystery

The Mystery in Washington, DC
The Canoe Trip Mystery
The Mystery of the Hidden Beach
The Mystery of the Missing Cat
The Mystery at Snowflake Inn
The Mystery on Stage
The Dinosaur Mystery
The Mystery of the Stolen Music
The Mystery at the Ball Park
The Chocolate Sundae Mystery
The Mystery of the Hot
   Air Balloon
The Mystery Bookstore
The Pilgrim Village Mystery
The Mystery of the Stolen
   Boxcar
The Mystery in the Cave
The Mystery on the Train
The Mystery at the Fair
The Mystery of the Lost Mine
The Guide Dog Mystery
The Hurricane Mystery
The Pet Shop Mystery
The Mystery of the Secret Message
The Firehouse Mystery
The Mystery in San Francisco
The Niagara Falls Mystery
The Mystery at the Alamo
The Outer Space Mystery
The Soccer Mystery
--- Old Attic

ER

The Panther Mystery
The Mystery of the Queen's Jewels
The Stolen Sword Mystery
The Basketball Mystery

D1473127

The Movie Star Mystery
The Mystery of the Pirate's Map
The Ghost Town Mystery
The Mystery of the Black Raven
The Mystery in the Mall
The Mystery in New York
The Gymnastics Mystery
The Poison Frog Mystery
The Mystery of the Empty Safe
The Home Run Mystery
The Great Bicycle Race Mystery
The Mystery of the Wild Ponies
The Mystery in the Computer
    Game
The Mystery at the Crooked
    House
The Hockey Mystery
The Mystery of the Midnight Dog
The Mystery of the Screech Owl
The Summer Camp Mystery
The Copycat Mystery
The Haunted Clock Tower
    Mystery
The Mystery of the Tiger's Eye
The Disappearing Staircase
    Mystery
The Mystery on Blizzard
    Mountain
The Mystery of the Spider's Clue
The Candy Factory Mystery
The Mystery of the Mummy's
    Curse
The Mystery of the Star Ruby
The Stuffed Bear Mystery
The Mystery of Alligator Swamp
The Mystery at Skeleton Point
The Tattletale Mystery
The Comic Book Mystery
The Great Shark Mystery
The Ice Cream Mystery
The Midnight Mystery

The Mystery in the Fortune
    Cookie
The Black Widow Spider Mystery
The Radio Mystery
The Mystery of the Runaway
    Ghost
The Finders Keepers Mystery
The Mystery of the Haunted
    Boxcar
The Clue in the Corn Maze
The Ghost of the Chattering
    Bones
The Sword of the Silver Knight
The Game Store Mystery
The Mystery of the Orphan Train
The Vanishing Passenger
The Giant Yo-Yo Mystery
The Creature in Ogopogo Lake
The Rock 'n' Roll Mystery
The Secret of the Mask
The Seattle Puzzle
The Ghost in the First Row
The Box That Watch Found
A Horse Named Dragon
The Great Detective Race
The Ghost at the Drive-In Movie
The Mystery of The Traveling
    Tomatoes
The Spy Game
The Dog-Gone Mystery
The Vampire Mystery
Superstar Watch
The Spy in the Bleachers
The Amazing Mystery Show

THE BOXCAR CHILDREN
SPOOKY SPECIAL

THE GHOST OF THE CHATTERING BONES
THE CREATURE IN OGOPOGO LAKE
THE VAMPIRE MYSTERY

created by
GERTRUDE CHANDLER WARNER

ALBERT WHITMAN & Company
Chicago, Illinois

The Boxcar Children Spooky Special
created by Gertrude Chandler Warner.

ISBN: 978-0-8075-0882-4

10 9 8 7 6 5 4 3 2 1 LB 15 14 13 12 11 10

Cover art by Robert Papp.

For information about Albert Whitman & Company,
visit our web site at www.albertwhitman.com.

THE GHOST OF THE CHATTERING BONES

created by
GERTRUDE CHANDLER WARNER

Illustrated by Robert Papp

The Ghost of the Chattering Bones
created by Gertrude Chandler Warner;
illustrated by Robert Papp.

ISBN 0-8075-0875-6 (hardcover)
ISBN 0-8075-0874-8 (paperback)

Cover art by Robert Papp.

For more information about Albert Whitman & Company,
visit our web site at www.albertwhitman.com.

Contents

CHAPTER   PAGE

1. The Haunted Bridge   1
2. A Strange Verse   16
3. The Watery Ghost!   32
4. Jon's Blunder   43
5. The Bones Chatter Again   56
6. Eton's Loop   69
7. Going . . . Going . . . Gone!   80
8. What's Wrong with This Picture?   90
9. Thief!   102
10. The Secret Hiding Place   113

Contents

Introduction vii

THE GHOST OF THE CHATTERING BONES

CHAPTER 1

The Haunted Bridge

"What kind of mystery is it, Mrs. McGregor?" asked six-year-old Benny. The youngest Alden couldn't keep still. He was bouncing up and down with excitement in the backseat of the family van.

Mrs. McGregor, who was sitting up front beside Grandfather Alden, looked over her shoulder and smiled. "It's Norah's story to tell, Benny," she said. "Not mine."

Henry gave his little brother a playful nudge. "Hold your horses, Benny," he said.

"It won't be long before we're at Eton Place." At fourteen, Henry was the oldest of the Aldens.

"I guess I can hold my horses a little bit longer," said Benny. He didn't like to wait.

Norah Eton, a good friend of the Aldens' housekeeper, had invited Mrs. McGregor and the four Alden children to come for a visit in the country. There was an old mystery that needed solving, and Henry, Jessie, Violet, and Benny were eager to hear all about it. There was nothing the Aldens liked better than a mystery. And together they'd managed to solve quite a few.

Twelve-year-old Jessie looked up from the map she was studying. "We make a left at the next road, Grandfather," she told him. Jessie was the best map reader in the family. She always knew how to get where they were going.

"Oh, now I remember!" Mrs. McGregor nodded. "It's been so long since I've been out this way, my memory's a bit foggy."

"How long has it been, Mrs. McGregor?" Grandfather Alden asked, as they turned off the highway onto a gravel road full of twists and turns.

"Let me see, now . . . Norah's great-niece, Pam, was just a toddler the last time I saw her," said Mrs. McGregor. She thought for a moment. "Now she would be about Violet's age."

At the mention of her name, ten-year-old Violet turned away from the window. "Will Pam be staying with her great-aunt Norah all summer?" she wanted to know.

"Oh, I imagine so," Mrs. McGregor answered. "She usually does. You see, her parents own an antique store in the city. They spend their summers traveling all over the country hunting for treasures."

Benny's eyebrows shot up. "Treasures?"

"Interesting old things to sell in their store," explained Mrs. McGregor. "They stop at every flea market and swap meet they can find."

That sounded like fun to Benny. "Why doesn't Pam go along?"

"Travel can be tiring," put in Grandfather, who often went away on business.

"Yes, indeed," agreed Mrs. McGregor.

"I imagine Pam would much rather spend her summers with her great-aunt Norah."

"That makes sense," said Henry.

Mrs. McGregor went on, "When Norah and I were young, we loved exploring Eton Place—all the fields and the streams and the woods. The property's been in the Eton family for a long time. As a matter of fact," she added, "Norah's putting together a history of the Eton family. She even hired a college student to help with the research."

"That must be interesting," said Jessie. "I'd like to put together a history of the Alden family sometime."

Benny tapped on his sister's shoulder to get her attention. "Don't forget to mention Watch, Jessie," he reminded her. Watch was the family dog.

"Oh, Benny!" Jessie laughed. "I'd never forget Watch."

"How about our boxcar?" asked Benny.

"I'd never forget our boxcar, either," Jessie told her little brother. "Our old home is an important part of our family history."

After their parents died, Jessie, Henry,

Benny, and Violet had run away. They found an old boxcar in the woods and stayed there for a while. Then James Alden found his grandchildren and brought them to live with him in his big white house in Greenfield. He even gave the boxcar a special place in the backyard. The children often used their former home as a clubhouse.

"I'm glad I brought my camera along," said Violet. "We can take pictures of our trip to go in our family history."

James Alden smiled into the rear view mirror. "Photos are a great way to keep a record of the times."

"I wonder what they did in the olden days," Jessie said thoughtfully, "before cameras were invented."

"They didn't have cameras back then?" Benny sounded surprised.

Violet shook her head. "Not until the 1820s." Violet knew a lot about photography. It was one of her hobbies.

"You're becoming a real expert, Violet," said Henry.

"Thanks, Henry." Violet beamed. "But

I still have a lot to learn."

Grandfather spotted a small gas station. He pulled up close to the gas pumps. A woman with gray streaks in her dark hair came over to the car.

"Fill 'er up?" the woman asked with a friendly smile. She was wearing blue overalls with the name DARLENE embroidered across the front.

Grandfather nodded. "You read my mind."

While Darlene filled the tank, the children hopped out of the car. They set to work washing the windows and the headlights.

"You folks on vacation?" Darlene asked them.

Jessie nodded. "We're spending a week in the country."

"Oh?"

"At Eton Place," Benny added.

As Darlene replaced the cap on the gas tank, she lowered her voice. "A word of advice," she said. "Don't go fishing from the old stone bridge. Some say it's haunted." Her eyes twinkled but her voice was serious.

The children were so surprised by Darlene's word that they were speechless. Before they had a chance to ask any questions, Grandfather had paid the bill and they were on their way again.

"Eton Place sounds a little . . . spooky," Benny said as they drove along.

"You don't believe there's really a ghost, do you?" Henry asked in his sensible way.

"Um, no," Benny said. But he didn't sound too sure.

Violet added, "Darlene was just teasing."

"I imagine she was talking about the ghost of the Chattering Bones," put in Mrs. McGregor.

The children all looked at their housekeeper in surprise. "The ghost of the what?" said Benny, his eyes round. "Did you say—"

"Oh, look!" Mrs. McGregor broke in, as the car rounded a curve. "There's the mailbox!"

Benny craned his neck. "Where?" he asked. He had been thinking about chattering bones. They were a scary thought.

Mrs. McGregor pointed to the side of the road. Sure enough, up ahead was a mailbox set atop a post. The shiny gold lettering on the side of the mailbox read: ETON PLACE.

Grandfather turned the station wagon into a long driveway that wound through the trees. They slowed to a stop when they came to a big plum-colored house with a large porch. On one side was an orchard. On the other, a flower garden.

"Oh, a purple house!" Violet cried with delight as she scooted sideways out of the wide backseat. Purple was Violet's favorite color. She almost always wore something purple or violet.

"Yes, the house has always been plum-colored," said Mrs. McGregor as Henry opened the car door for her. "Thanks to Meg Plum."

As Grandfather lifted the suitcases out of the car, Jessie noticed a tall, silver-haired woman in a flowery-blue sundress standing near the orchard. She was talking to a man in a business suit. As if feeling Jessie's eyes on her, the woman suddenly looked over.

"Margaret!" The tall woman rushed towards Mrs. McGregor. "How wonderful to see you!"

"It's been too long," said Mrs. McGregor, returning her friend's warm hug.

"And this fine-looking group must be the Alden family!" Norah Eton said.

Mrs. McGregor proudly introduced everyone. "Welcome to Eton Place!" Norah said, a smile spreading across her face. "I can't wait for you to meet my niece. I know she'll enjoy your company."

"We're looking forward to meeting Pam," said Jessie, speaking for them all.

"Guess what, Mrs. Eton?" Benny put in. He was still thinking about the mystery.

"What, Benny?"

"We're pretty good at tracking down clues," he told her proudly.

"So I've heard," said Norah. "I'll tell you all about the old mystery after dinner, Benny. But you have to promise me one thing."

"All right," said Benny. "What is it?"

"You must call me Norah."

"Okay, Norah," agreed Benny. "It's a deal!"

Just then, a voice boomed out. "I'm Spence Morton." The man in the business suit walked toward the group and put out his hand for Grandfather to shake. "I hope you're not here about the bridge, too," he said. "I made a fair offer, but I'll go higher if necessary."

Henry, Jessie, Violet, and Benny looked at each other in bewilderment. Was this the same bridge Darlene had mentioned?

Spence Morton went on, "I was passing through town and happened to pick up a local paper." He pulled a newspaper out from under his arm and thumped a finger under a picture of an old stone bridge. "This is exactly what I've been looking for!" he told them, his eyes glittering behind gold-rimmed glasses. "My wife takes great pride in her English garden," he added, "and this charming bridge will be perfect for the stream that runs through it."

"That bridge is not for sale," Norah stated icily. "As I said before, you're wasting your time."

The man did not look pleased to hear this. "Everything has a price tag," he insisted.

"We'll see about that." Norah's mouth was set in a thin, hard line.

"Mark my words," said Spence Morton, "I'll do whatever it takes to get what I want." With that, he turned and walked away.

Norah sighed. "Every time I turn around lately, there's Spence Morton. Yesterday I found him measuring my bridge! Can you believe it?"

Mrs. McGregor shook her head. "The nerve!"

"He isn't a bad person, but..." Norah stopped and let out a long sigh.

"But," finished Grandfather, "he just won't take no for an answer."

Norah nodded slowly. "I wish now I'd never let the newspaper do that write-up on my bridge." Then, changing the subject, she added, "Will you join us for a late dinner, James? There's plenty to go around."

"Thanks, Norah," he said, "but the sun's already going down, and I still have some business to take care of."

Grandfather gave a cheery honk as he drove away. Everyone waved, then headed toward the plum-colored house.

Mrs. McGregor looked around as they stepped inside. She smiled at Norah. "I see you've made some changes," she said.

"Yes, I finally got around to fixing the house up a bit," said Norah. As she led the way to the stairs, she shook her head. "But what a mess! Walls torn down...floorboards pulled up. This place was a real disaster area for a while."

Upstairs, a room with plum-patterned wallpaper was waiting for Mrs. McGregor, another with fan-shaped windows for Violet and Jessie. A third bedroom with twin beds and fringed blue bedspreads was just right for Henry and Benny.

"We've been keeping dinner warm for you," Norah told them. "Anybody hungry?"

Benny waved his hand in the air. "I am!

I am!" he cried, to no one's surprise. The youngest Alden was always hungry.

Norah laughed. "Well, come on down as soon as you've settled in."

It didn't take the Aldens long to unpack. They were waiting for Violet to finish brushing her hair when Benny cried, "Look!" He was peering through one of the fan-shaped windows.

Jessie could tell by her little brother's face that something had startled him. "What's going on, Benny?" she asked, stepping up beside him.

"Look down there!" Benny said, his eyes wide.

"What is it?" Henry hurried over, with Violet close behind.

"It's a bridge!" declared Benny.

The Aldens huddled around, straining to see out into the gathering darkness. Sure enough, the shadowy outline of a curved stone bridge could be seen in a far corner of the backyard.

"There must be a creek behind the house," noted Henry.

Violet said, "I can't be sure, but I think

that's the bridge that was in the newspaper."

"Got to be," said Jessie. "That's the one Spence Morton wants to buy. I'm sure of it."

Benny nodded. "I bet it's the haunted bridge Darlene was talking about. We're not supposed to go fishing from it, remember?"

"Of course we can go fishing from it, Benny," Henry insisted. "The bridge isn't haunted."

"No one goes fishing from that bridge," said a voice behind them. "No one does. Ever."

CHAPTER 2

A Strange Verse

Henry, Jessie, Violet, and Benny turned around quickly in surprise. A young girl about Violet's age was standing at the opened door, watching them. She was wearing jeans and a green T-shirt. Her blond curls were held back from her face with a beaded headband.

"You must be Pam," Jessie said with a friendly smile.

"That's right. And you must be the Aldens."

"Yes. I'm Jessie, and this is Henry, Benny,

and Violet." Jessie motioned to her brothers and sister in turn.

"I don't get it," said Henry. "Why doesn't anyone go fishing from—"

Before Henry could finish his thought, Pam wheeled around and walked off.

The Aldens looked at one another in confusion. "Pam sure seemed in a hurry to get away," Violet said with a puzzled frown.

"I guess she didn't want to talk about the bridge," said Jessie. "I wonder why."

Henry shrugged. "Beats me."

"I bet it *is* haunted," Benny said in a hushed voice. "I just bet!"

* * * *

"Help yourself to more meatballs, Benny," Norah urged at dinner.

The youngest Alden didn't need to be coaxed. "Thanks," he said, eagerly adding a few more to his plate of spaghetti.

Mrs. McGregor turned to Norah's great-niece. "You've really grown since I saw you last, Pam," she said with a warm smile.

"Time sure flies, doesn't it?" Norah took the basket of garlic bread that Violet handed her. "Pam was only a toddler when she spent her first summer with me." Norah reached out and gave her niece an affectionate pat on the arm.

Violet looked over at Pam. "You must miss your parents."

Pam's face turned red and she lowered her eyes.

"We miss Grandfather whenever he goes away on business," Benny chimed in as he wiped tomato sauce from his chin.

Pam looked glumly at her plate. "Who needs parents around all the time?"

The Aldens were surprised by her words, but they didn't say anything.

Just then, a young woman in a yellow halter top and matching shorts came into the room. She was very tall with lots of curly brown hair. "Sorry I'm late, Norah," she said, slipping into an empty chair beside Jessie. "I lose all track of time when I'm working."

"Not to worry," Norah said with a cheery smile. "Everything's still piping hot." Then she introduced Mrs. McGregor and the Aldens to Annette Tanning. "Annette's helping me research the Eton family. She's from out-of-state, so she'll be staying here until school starts again in the fall."

"You're in college, Annette?" Jessie asked, passing the salad along.

"Yes, I'm studying history." Annette placed a napkin over her lap. "When I saw Norah's ad for a research assistant, I jumped at it."

Norah smiled. "I was lucky to get such a hard worker."

"I really love looking through old things," Annette went on. "You never know what treasures you'll find."

That got Benny's attention. "You found a treasure?"

"Not a real treasure." Annette laughed nervously. "Nothing like that. Just interesting facts. That's all I meant about—" She stopped suddenly as if she knew she'd said too much.

Benny polished off his milk. "We're good at finding real treasures," he said proudly. "Right, Henry?"

"We have found a few," Henry admitted.

Seeing Annette's puzzled face, Mrs. McGregor explained, "These children are first-class detectives."

"Detectives?" Pam looked over in surprise.

"We solve mysteries," Benny told her with a grin. "That's our specialty."

Norah turned to her assistant. "I think we have just the mystery for them. Right, Annette?"

"What...?" Annette held her fork in mid-air. "What are you talking about?" She sounded upset.

"Why, Meg Plum's mystery, of course," answered Norah. "What else?"

Suddenly Annette's whole manner changed. "If you don't think *I'm* doing a good job, Norah, just say so!" She stabbed at a meatball with her fork.

The Aldens were surprised. They stared at Annette with their mouths open.

"Of course I think you're doing a good job." Norah looked shocked. "What's gotten into you, Annette?"

"Well, for starters, I can't work with a

bunch of kids in the way."

Benny put down his fork. "But we never get in the way."

Mrs. McGregor was quick to agree. "The Aldens are very self-reliant."

"Of course they are," agreed Norah. "No reason for anyone to be upset." But it was clear that Annette was upset.

"We'll do our best to help," Henry promised.

"Thank you, Henry," said Norah.

Annette looked as if she wanted to argue. But she didn't. She finished her dinner in silence, not looking too pleased. Then she excused herself and left the room.

Norah apologized for her assistant's behavior. "Annette has many good qualities, but she can be a bit moody sometimes."

When the Aldens were clearing the table, Henry let out a low whistle. "Annette sure doesn't want us helping out," he said.

Benny added, "She wasn't very friendly."

"I guess we'd better keep out of her way," said Jessie, filling the sink with hot, soapy water. The children agreed.

After leaving the kitchen spic-and-span, the four Alden children hurried out to the front porch. Norah and Mrs. McGregor were sipping iced tea and chatting. Pam was bent over a jigsaw puzzle nearby. Annette was nowhere in sight.

The Aldens made themselves comfortable. Then Benny looked at Norah—was she ready to tell them about the mystery?

Norah was ready. She took a last sip of her iced tea, then placed the empty glass on the table beside her. In the soft glow of the porch light, with the crickets singing in the dark, she began telling them an odd tale.

"A long time ago, my great-great-grandfather, Jon Eton, decided to see a bit of the world. His travels took him to England, and to the little village of Stone Pool. That's where he met and fell in love with the beautiful Meg Plum."

"That's why your house is purple, right?" put in Violet. "Because of Meg Plum, I mean."

Norah looked surprised that Violet knew that. "Right you are, Violet," she said.

"Meg left the village of Stone Pool behind to start a new life with Jon right here at Eton Place. But I'm afraid my great-great-grandmother didn't have an easy time of it."

Jessie looked questioningly at Norah. "You mean, she didn't like it here?"

"Oh, she liked it well enough, Jessie. But she was terribly homesick. Apparently, she would sit for hours, just staring at a photograph of Stone Pool." Norah shook her head sadly. "They say Jon often found his young wife in tears."

"Poor Meg!" Violet was shy, and meeting new people often made her nervous. "Did Jon try to help her?"

"Yes, but I'll tell you about that another time, Violet." Norah was reaching for a photograph album from the table beside her. "Right now, I have something to show you. It just so happens Annette came across a photograph the other day." She pointed at a page in the album. "Here it is—Meg's photograph of the village of Stone Pool."

Although it was cracked and badly faded with age, the photograph showed shoppers

in old-fashioned clothes strolling along the walkways and in and out of the little stores. Benny pointed to the fancy script at the bottom of the photo.

"What does that say, Norah?" he wanted to know. The youngest Alden was just learning to read.

Norah put on her glasses and read the words aloud: "The village of Stone Pool as it appeared on a summer afternoon in 1810."

Mrs. McGregor peered over Norah's shoulder. "Looks like a charming village. No wonder Meg was homesick."

Norah continued her story. "One day, a special gift arrived for Meg from her grandmother."

The Aldens were instantly curious. "What was it?" said Henry.

"A heart-shaped brooch," Norah told them. "It was a family heirloom made from precious gems. The rubies were particularly beautiful and rare."

"What's a brooch?" asked Benny.

"It's a pin, Benny," Mrs. McGregor

answered. "Just like the one I have on my blouse. Only Meg's brooch sounds much fancier than mine."

"Meg loved the brooch. She wore it whenever she was feeling homesick." Norah started flipping through the pages of her album again. She stopped and pulled out an old photograph. "Here's a picture of my great-great-grandmother wearing her brooch." She passed it along.

Sure enough, the fair-haired woman in the high-necked blouse and long skirt was wearing a heart-shaped brooch at her throat. The Aldens took turns studying it— first Violet, then Benny, then Henry, and finally Jessie.

"I wish I could show you the brooch itself," said Norah, taking the photograph that Jessie handed her. "But I'm afraid that's impossible."

"Impossible?" Jessie looked puzzled.

Norah let out a sigh. "Sadly, the brooch disappeared long ago."

"Oh, no!" cried Violet.

"Apparently, Meg left the heart-shaped

brooch on her dresser one evening," Norah explained. "In the morning, it was gone."

Benny's mouth dropped open. "You mean . . . somebody stole it?"

"That's what everybody figured," said Norah. "But the strange thing is, they say there was no sign that someone had broken into the house."

"There's something I don't understand," Henry remarked. "Why would Meg leave a valuable heirloom out on her dresser in the first place?"

Jessie had been wondering the same thing. "If the brooch meant so much to her, why didn't Meg put it away in a safe place?"

"Exactly—yes!" said Norah, who seemed delighted by their questions. "It doesn't make sense, does it?"

Henry raised an eyebrow. "What are you saying, Norah?"

"I'm saying that I don't think the brooch was stolen." Norah closed the album and placed it on the table beside her. "I've always believed Meg found a secret hiding place for it."

Jessie blinked in surprise. "Why would she do something like that?"

"It's not as strange as you might think, Jessie." Norah settled back against a cushion. "I'm just guessing, but it's possible she hid that brooch to keep it safe—and out of her husband's reach."

"What do you mean?" asked Violet.

"Now, don't get me wrong," Norah said, holding up a hand. "Jon Eton was a kind man, but he liked to gamble. He was a bit too interested in money for his own good."

"Interested enough to sell Meg's brooch?" Jessie asked in surprise.

"It's hard to say, Jessie. But I don't think Meg was taking any chances. I'm convinced she found a hiding place for it."

"How can you be so sure, Norah?" Henry wondered.

"Because in her later years, Meg made a wall-hanging with a verse hand-stitched on it." Norah leaned forward. "I believe that verse holds a secret."

"What kind of secret, Norah?" asked Henry, unable to keep the excitement out of his voice.

"The secret of where the brooch is hidden." Norah reached down for the framed verse propped against her chair.

"Oh, it's beautiful!" Violet cried as Norah held it up for everyone to see.

Jessie moved closer to get a better look. "Meg used a different-colored thread for every letter," she said admiringly.

Norah smiled proudly. "Meg was known for her fancy stitching."

Benny could hardly stand the suspense. "What does it say, Norah?" he asked, bouncing up and down. "The verse, I mean."

Norah smiled at Benny's enthusiasm. Then she read the words on it aloud:

> *When last goes first,*
> *and first goes last,*
> *Eton's Loop will show you*
> *a clue from the past.*

Confused, the Aldens looked at one another. After hearing the verse one more time, Henry said, "That's a tough one to figure out!"

Benny agreed. "It's not much to go on."

Jessie tugged her small notebook and pencil from her pocket. As she copied the verse, Henry and Violet looked at each other and smiled. They could always count on Jessie to be organized.

"I don't get it." Benny was thinking hard. "What exactly is Eton's Loop?"

"I wish I knew, Benny," Norah told him.

"When we were your age," put in Mrs. McGregor, "we drove ourselves crazy trying to figure it out. Every time we thought we were on to something—"

"We'd end up going around in circles!" finished Norah.

Violet had a sudden thought. "Would you like to work on the mystery with us, Pam?" she asked, looking over at her.

"We can use all the help we can get," added Henry.

Pam shook her head. "I don't like mysteries," she said, barely looking up from her puzzle.

Benny could hardly believe his ears. "But they're just like jigsaw puzzles," he was quick to point out. "You fit all the pieces together and—"

Before he had a chance to finish, Pam suddenly got to her feet. "I think I'll go up to bed."

Norah looked disappointed. "Well . . . I suppose that's best if you're tired. Oh, would you mind putting this back in the living room for me on your way, dear?" she added, holding the photograph album out to Pam.

"In the cabinet with the glass doors, right?"

"Right."

With that, Pam gave her great-aunt a hug, then she said good-night and went inside. Norah looked worried.

"Pam just hasn't been herself this summer," she said. "She's usually so cheery. For the life of me, I can't figure out what's bothering her."

The Aldens looked at one another, wondering the same thing.

CHAPTER 3

The Watery Ghost

That night, all the Aldens fell asleep right away. Around midnight, Benny stirred. He thought he heard something— a rushing kind of sound. It seemed to be coming from outside. What was making that noise?

"Henry?" he whispered.

Henry didn't answer. He was sound asleep.

Benny slid out of bed. He went over to the window. Leaning on the sill, he peered out through the window screen into the inky darkness.

The strange noise suddenly stopped.

"Benny?" Henry asked sleepily. "What's going on?"

"I . . . I heard something."

"It's just the crickets," Henry said in the middle of a yawn. "Nothing to worry about."

Benny nodded his head. "No, it was something else, Henry," he insisted, trying to keep his voice low. "Something . . . weird."

"You were probably dreaming," Henry told him, in a sleepy voice.

"Maybe," Benny said, as he climbed back into bed. But he knew he wasn't dreaming.

* * * *

"I'm telling you, your great-great-grandmother's brooch was stolen," Annette was telling Norah at breakfast the next morning. "If you ask me, it was taken by one of the workmen at the time."

Benny frowned. "You don't think there's a secret hiding place?"

"I certainly don't." Annette tore a small piece of crust off her toast and popped it into her mouth. "I've done the research. I know what I'm talking about."

Benny looked crushed.

Violet felt her little brother's disappointment. "We won't know for sure until we do some investigating, Benny." She passed the platter of bacon to Pam.

Henry nodded. "We should at least check into it."

"Maybe you missed something, Annette," Benny said.

This was the wrong thing to say. Annette frowned. "Well, isn't it lucky we have the Aldens around to keep us on track," she said, though it was clear from her voice that she didn't think it was lucky at all.

Jessie and Henry looked at each other. Why was Annette so unfriendly?

"According to all the old newspapers, there was no evidence of theft." Norah took a bite of her toast and chewed thoughtfully. "And what about that little verse of Meg's? What do you think it means, Annette?"

"Nothing, probably."

Norah lifted an eyebrow. "Nothing?"

"Nonsense verse," Annette said, patting her mouth with a napkin. "That's all it is."

Pam tucked a loose strand of hair under her polka-dotted headband. "What's nonsense verse?" she asked.

"A silly rhyme that has no meaning whatsoever," Annette answered.

But Norah wasn't convinced. "I think there's more to Meg's verse than meets the eye."

Mrs. McGregor was quick to agree. "If anyone can figure it out, the Aldens can."

Annette threw up her hands in a frustrated way. "Well, I have better things to do with my time," she said, pushing back her chair. "I'll be in the den if you need me."

"Before you go, Annette," Norah said, changing the subject. "I was wondering if you've seen my tape recorder. It seems to have disappeared from my desk."

Jessie couldn't help noticing that Pam was blushing.

"I'm afraid not," said Annette. Then an

amused smile curled her lips. "But I'm sure the Aldens can track it down—just like that!" she added, with a snap of her fingers. Then she hurried away.

"I don't think Annette likes us," Benny said in a small voice. He wasn't used to anyone making fun of them.

"I'm sure she likes you just fine, Benny," Norah assured him. "She puts in long hours and it makes her a bit grumpy. You mustn't let it bother you." She paused as she swallowed a mouthful of eggs. "This research seems to mean a great deal to Annette. I'm not really sure why."

Mrs. McGregor, who was buttering her toast, suddenly looked up. "Your assistant seems sure the brooch was stolen."

Benny nodded. "By one of the workmen. I wonder what she meant by that."

"She was talking about the men who were working on the bridge," explained Norah, as she poured syrup on her pancakes. "They were hired around the time the brooch disappeared."

Henry asked, "Are you talking about the

bridge out back?"

"That's right, Henry," said Norah. "It came all the way from Stone Pool."

"Stone Pool?" Violet looked at Norah in surprise.

"It was the bridge where Jon proposed to Meg," put in Mrs. McGregor, as she helped herself to more bacon. "Right, Norah?"

Norah smiled at her friend. "Yes, indeed, Margaret! And Jon was determined to bring that bridge across the ocean for his bride."

Violet nodded in understanding. Jon wanted to bring a part of Stone Pool to Eton Place to keep Meg from feeling homesick.

"They say he made an offer that the village of Stone Pool just couldn't refuse. In no time at all, the bridge was taken apart, stone by stone, and shipped to America." Norah smiled a little. "There was only one problem."

"What was that, Norah?" Jessie asked.

"Jon was positive the bridge would span the stream in the woods," she said. "But he was sadly mistaken. You see, the bridge wasn't nearly long enough."

"At least the bridge was the right size for the stream behind the house," Violet pointed out.

"There's no stream running through the backyard, Violet." Norah said. "The bridge doesn't cross over water—only a large bed of pansies."

"No wonder nobody ever goes fishing from it," Henry realized.

"Not a drop of water under it," Norah said with a nod. "Never has been." She handed the syrup to Benny. "But Meg didn't mind," she added. "It made her happy to look out and see that old stone bridge in the backyard."

Benny was wondering about something. "Is the bridge haunted, Norah?"

"Darlene spilled the beans, I'm afraid," said Mrs. McGregor.

Norah rolled her eyes. "Darlene never did know how to hold her tongue."

The Aldens looked at one another in astonishment. Had Darlene been right after all?

"Does Jon haunt the bridge?" Violet wanted to know. "Or is it Meg?"

Benny suddenly remembered what Mrs. McGregor had said. "I bet it's the ghost of the chattering bones!"

Norah smiled over at the youngest Alden. "You hit the nail on the head, Benny!"

Jessie was curious. "Will you tell us more about it, Norah?"

Norah said, "Over the years strange noises have sometimes been heard in the middle of the night."

Benny's eyes widened. "What kind of noises?"

"I've never heard the noises myself, Benny," Norah said, as she padded her mouth with a napkin. "But they say it sounds just like water flowing over rocks."

The Aldens were so surprised all they could do was stare. Before they could ask any questions, Norah spoke again.

"You see, 'Chattering Bones' was the name of a little stream near Stone Pool. For many years it flowed under an old stone bridge on the edge of town."

Violet gasped. "The bridge Jon bought for Meg?"

Norah nodded her head. "The very same one that was taken apart and shipped across the ocean."

Pam, who had been quietly peeling an orange, suddenly looked up. "Just after that, the Chattering Bones disappeared."

"Disappeared?" the Aldens echoed in unison.

Pam nodded. "It vanished into thin air."

Henry was baffled. "But it couldn't just . . . vanish!"

"Apparently it did, Henry. They say the stream dried up shortly after the bridge was torn down. It was almost as if the creek needed the bridge." Norah spoke slowly as if uncertain about what she was saying.

Violet shivered. Everything was becoming more and more mysterious. Benny's eyes were round. "You mean, the sound at night is the ghost of the Chattering Bones?"

Pam was the first to answer. "Yes, the ghostly stream flows under the bridge when it's dark." Her voice was quiet, almost a whisper.

Benny's eyes grew even rounder. He hurried over to the window and peeked outside.

"That's a strange ghost story," Jessie remarked, as she got up to clear the table.

"Eton Place has its share of mysteries," Mrs. McGregor agreed. "No doubt about that."

Benny suddenly looked over at Norah. "That man's out there again."

"What man?" asked Henry, coming up behind his brother.

"The one who wants to buy the bridge."

In a flash, Norah was on her feet. "That fellow needs to be told a thing or two!"

Everyone followed as she led the way outside. Sure enough, they found Spence Morton standing on the bridge. He waved over to them. Spence was all smiles when they hurried over. "Just checking on my bridge," he told them.

"Now just what does that mean?" Norah had an angry frown on her face.

But Spence didn't seem to hear Norah. He just stared down at the stones and smiled.

"This bridge is mine," Norah said sharply. "And I won't be selling it to you or anyone else!"

Spence suddenly laughed, but not in a funny way. "I've got a hunch you'll change your mind," he said. Then he turned and strode away.

The Aldens exchanged worried looks. What was Spence Morton planning to do?

CHAPTER 4

Jon's Blunder

As Spence walked off, Benny edged closer to the rough stone ledge and peered over the side. Down below, purple pansies rippled in the breeze. He looked relieved.

As if reading his thoughts, Henry put a comforting arm around his brother. "Not a drop of water in sight."

"The Chattering Bones haunts the bridge at night," said Pam, who was standing within earshot. "Remember?"

Henry turned to look at her. "You don't really believe that, do you?"

Before Pam had a chance to answer, Jessie called out, "Look at this." She pointed to a small bronze plaque bolted to one of the stones. Engraved on the plaque were the words JON'S BLUNDER.

"One of the men working on the bridge had it made as a joke," Norah told them. "It wasn't long before everyone started calling the bridge Jon's Blunder."

Benny frowned. "What's a blunder?"

"A blunder's a mistake, Benny," Henry told him. "A big mistake."

"Oh!" said Benny, catching on. "And Jon made a big mistake—the bridge wasn't long enough for the stream."

Norah laughed. "I'm afraid my great-great-grandfather never heard the end of it."

Just then, Violet noticed something, too. The shape of a heart had been chiseled into one of the stones nearby. In the middle of the heart was Meg's name.

They all moved closer for a better look. "Jon carved that heart for Meg on the day he proposed to her," said Mrs. McGregor. "Right, Norah?"

"That's right, Margaret."

"It's so romantic," said Violet. She had a dreamy smile on her face as she traced the letters MEG with a finger.

But Benny was more interested in the mystery. "Let's get started looking for clues," he suggested.

"Any idea where you'll begin?" Norah asked as they headed back to the house.

"We thought we'd hike around the property," said Jessie. "Maybe keep an eye out for Eton's Loop."

"Whatever that is," added Benny.

Mrs. McGregor looked up at the blue sky. "Why not pack a lunch?" she suggested.

"Oh, yes!" put in Norah. "What could be better than a picnic?"

"Nothing!" cried Benny, who loved picnics.

Mrs. McGregor smiled. "There's a great spot to eat by the stream in the woods."

"Sounds good," said Henry.

"Come with us, Pam," Jessie offered.

Pam put on a little smile. "Thanks, but

I never hike that far. Not all the way to the woods."

The Aldens looked at each other, puzzled. How could anyone turn down a picnic?

As they went inside, Norah said, "By the way, there's a potluck dinner at the community center tonight, so watch the time."

"What's a—" Benny began to say, but Jessie knew the question before he asked it.

"A potluck's where everybody brings something, Benny," she explained. "That way, you get to sample different dishes."

Benny broke into a big grin. "Sounds like fun!"

"A picnic and a potluck dinner in the same day," said Henry. "That's a dream come true for you, Benny!"

The Aldens washed and dried the breakfast dishes, then made sandwiches on the counter. Violet buttered the bread. Henry added cold cuts, pickles, and lettuce. Benny slapped on the mustard. And Jessie cut and wrapped the sandwiches that Benny passed to her.

"I wonder why Pam never wants to do anything with us," said Benny, licking some mustard from the back of his hand.

"I'm not sure," Jessie said after a moment's thought. "She's hard to figure out."

"You've got that right," said Henry.

"She didn't even want to help us solve a mystery," added Benny, who still couldn't get over it.

"Maybe Pam's shy around new people," Violet was quick to suggest.

Jessie frowned as she wrapped a sandwich. She thought there was more to it than that. Pam always seemed so eager to get away from them.

Henry filled a large thermos with lemonade. "I think we should concentrate on one mystery at a time," he said, and the others nodded.

Jessie loaded their picnic lunch into her backpack. She even remembered Benny's special cup—the cracked pink cup he had found while they were living in the boxcar.

Then they filed out the door.

"Stick together!" Norah called out to

them from an opened window. "We don't want anyone to get lost."

"Don't worry, Norah," Jessie called back to her with a little wave. "We always stick together."

The Aldens set off across the fields, following a row of scraggly pines that grew near a rail fence. They made a detour around a weedy pond and stopped by a lone apple tree on a hill to pick wildflowers. By the time they reached the woods, the afternoon sun was getting hot and their flowers were starting to wilt.

"I'm starving," said Benny, as they followed a winding path covered with pine needles. "Is it lunchtime yet?"

"Got to be!" said Henry. "I'm ready for a break."

"Mrs. McGregor said there was a good spot for a picnic by the stream," Violet recalled.

"It must be up ahead," guessed Jessie. "Let's keep going a while longer."

Pine needles crackled under Benny's feet as he quickened his pace. "Sure hope we find it soon," he said, rubbing his empty stomach.

"Doesn't it smell wonderful here?" Violet said, looking back at her older sister.

Jessie filled her lungs with the spicy scent of pine. "It sure does."

Just then, Benny stopped so quickly that Henry almost bumped into him.

"What's wrong?" Henry asked.

Benny stood frozen to the spot.

"Benny?" Jessie said in alarm. "Are you okay?"

The youngest Alden put a finger to his lips signaling for the others to be quiet. "Listen!"

No one spoke for a moment. Then Henry nodded. So did Jessie and Violet. They heard it, too. A rushing noise.

"That's water rushing over rocks," stated Henry. "The stream must be close by."

It wasn't long before they reached a stream that wound its way through the woods.

They quickly made themselves comfortable on the grassy bank. Then Jessie passed out the sandwiches while Henry poured the lemonade.

"Mrs. McGregor was right," Violet said as she unwrapped a sandwich. "This really is a perfect spot for a picnic."

Jessie looked around. "It's a perfect spot for a bridge, too," she said, taking the lemonade that Henry handed her.

"You're right, Jessie," said Henry. "I bet this is just where Jon Eton was going to put that old stone bridge."

"I wonder if . . . " Violet began and then stopped herself.

"Are you wondering if one of the workmen really did steal Meg's brooch?" Jessie asked. "I don't blame you, Violet. I can't help wondering about that myself."

"Annette seems so convinced," said Violet.

Henry suddenly had a thought that hadn't occurred to him before. "Maybe it wasn't one of the workmen who stole the brooch."

"What are you getting at, Henry?" Violet looked confused.

"Maybe Jon took Meg's brooch."

"I suppose so." Violet frowned. She didn't want to believe Jon Eton would steal his wife's family heirloom.

"If only we could figure out Meg's verse," said Jessie. She pulled her notebook from her back pocket and read the words aloud one more time.

> *When last goes first,*
> *and first goes last,*
> *Eton's Loop will show you*
> *a clue from the past.*

But nobody had any idea what the verse meant. It still didn't make any sense.

Violet couldn't help noticing that her little brother was unusually quiet. She could tell something was troubling him. "Is anything wrong, Benny?"

Benny's eyes were fixed on the water flowing swiftly over the rocks. "I heard it last night," he said softly.

"Heard what, Benny?" Jessie asked.

"Water rushing over rocks!"

The others stopped eating and stared at him. "I didn't know what it was," Benny told them. "But now I do."

"You couldn't have heard this stream last night, Benny," Henry argued. "It's too far away from the house."

Benny shook his head. "It wasn't this stream, Henry. It was the ghost—the ghost of the Chattering Bones!"

"Oh!" Violet put one hand over her mouth in surprise.

But Henry wasn't having any of that. "There's no such thing as ghosts, Benny," he said for the umpteenth time. "Not even ghost streams."

Violet glanced at Henry. She knew her older brother was right. And yet, Benny's words still gave her a chill.

"Benny, are you sure you weren't dreaming?" Jessie wanted to know.

"I thought maybe I was," Benny admitted. "I even forgot all about the weird noise for a while—until we got closer to this stream." He looked over at his brother and sisters. "It wasn't a dream last night. I'm sure of it."

"There's only one way to settle this," said Jessie. "If it happens again, we'll all check it out together."

Violet added, "That's a promise."

"There must be an explanation for what you heard, Benny," said Henry. "We just have to figure out what it is."

Benny gave his brother and sisters a grateful smile. They always knew how to make him feel better.

After lunch, the four Aldens slipped off their socks and shoes and stood ankle-deep in the icy cold stream. The water was so clear they could see to the bottom. Side-stepping the rocks, they waded downstream. By the time they got back, their pockets were bulging with interesting pebbles.

When they stepped onto the mossy bank again, Violet spotted something half-hidden in the long grass nearby. "Look at this," she said, holding up a braided green headband.

"I bet somebody's looking all over for that," said Jessie.

"Pam always wears headbands," Benny pointed out as he put on his socks.

Henry nodded. "Maybe it's hers."

"Possibly," said Jessie. "But not likely."

Violet agreed. "Pam never hikes this far, remember?" She slipped the headband into her pocket, hoping to find the owner.

Henry looked at his watch. "I guess we should head back."

"Right," said Jessie, remembering the potluck dinner. "It's a long hike."

With that, the four children followed the path out of the woods, still no closer to solving the mystery. In fact, they didn't have the faintest idea how they were going to solve it. All they knew was that they had to try.

CHAPTER 5

The Bones Chatter Again

Benny was checking himself out in the hall mirror when Mrs. McGregor came down the stairs in a peach-colored dress. "Doesn't everyone look wonderful!" she said, smiling fondly at the children.

Henry, Jessie, Violet, and Benny were ready for the potluck dinner. Jessie was wearing a watermelon-pink dress with pearly buttons. Violet had changed into a lavender T-shirt and pale blue skirt with lace pockets. Henry wore a blue shirt and black pants. And Benny had on a short-sleeved white shirt and tan pants.

Just then, Pam came out of the kitchen holding a covered dish. The cream-colored headband in her hair matched her dress. Norah, in a ruffled blue dress, was right behind her.

"Pam made pasta salad for the potluck," Norah said proudly as they headed out to the car.

"Oh, do you enjoy cooking, Pam?" Violet asked.

Pam nodded. "I'm not very good at it yet," she said. "But I'm learning."

"Pam's being modest," Mrs. McGregor said as they pulled out of the driveway. "It just so happens I had a taste—and it was delicious!"

"It smells delicious!" Benny piped up from the backseat.

Pam, who was sitting up front between her great-aunt and Mrs. McGregor, turned around and smiled. "I'm making cookies tomorrow, Benny. You can help me decorate them if you want."

"Sure!" Benny was grinning from ear to ear.

Pam was being very nice to Benny,

Jessie thought.

"I was hoping Annette would join us," Norah said as they drove through the peaceful countryside. "She doesn't know a soul around here. I wanted to introduce her to a few people, but she said she'd rather work."

"You certainly have a dedicated assistant," Mrs. McGregor remarked.

Norah nodded, then she added, "By the way, if anyone comes across that tape recorder of mine, please let me know right away. Annette and I both use it for research."

"You mean, it's still missing, Norah?" Mrs. McGregor was surprised to hear this.

"I'm afraid so."

"We'll keep an eye out for it," Jessie promised. And the others nodded.

"Oh, Pam," Violet said, "speaking of lost things, are you missing a headband? A braided green headband?"

Pam whirled around. "Yes, did you find it?"

Violet nodded. "We came across it when we were out today."

"That's great!" said Pam. "It's my favorite."

The Aldens looked at each other. Pam said she never went into the woods. Why would she lie to them?

Just then, Norah pulled into the busy parking lot at the community center. "I wonder what everybody's bringing for the potluck," said Benny. He sounded excited.

"One thing's for sure," said Norah, parking in an empty space. "You'll be stuffed to the gills by the time we leave!"

Benny jumped out of the car. "Let's go," he said, heading for the door.

Henry laughed. "When it comes to food, there's no stopping Benny."

Inside the packed center, people were already helping themselves to the hot and cold food set out on a long table. Pam went over to add her dish to the others.

"Wow, there sure are a lot of potluckers here," Benny said as he looked around. "I hope they save some food for us."

Jessie smiled at her little brother and brushed her fingers across his hair. "Don't worry, Benny. I'm sure there's plenty to go around."

Norah put a hand to her cheek. "Oh, no. There he is again!" she said, keeping her voice low.

The Aldens and Mrs. McGregor looked at Norah, then in the direction she was staring. A man in gold-rimmed glasses was eating dinner at a small table in the corner. The man was Spence Morton!

"Never mind, now. We'll just keep out of his way," Mrs. McGregor told her friend.

Henry noticed that Benny was eyeing the buffet table again. "I think there's still plenty of food there, Benny," he teased.

Norah smiled at the youngest Alden. "Getting hungry?"

"Sort of," Benny said, looking at her expectantly. "Is it time to eat yet?"

Norah laughed. "Go ahead."

The Aldens quickly made their way over to the buffet while Norah and Mrs. McGregor mingled with the other guests. The children followed the line of people moving slowly around the table. After helping themselves to the different dishes, they carried their heaping plates to a small table and sat down.

"Mmm," said Jessie, digging in. "Have you tried Pam's pasta salad? It really is great."

Henry nodded. "I'll second that."

"Don't all look at once," said Violet, "but Spence Morton has company."

One by one, the other Aldens peeked over to take a look. Someone with gray streaks in her dark hair was sitting across from Spence. They seemed to be deep in conversation.

"Isn't that Darlene?" Jessie said in surprise, trying not to stare.

"You mean the lady from the gas station?" asked Benny.

Violet turned around slowly to take another glance. "Yes, I think you're right, Jessie."

"I wonder what that's all about," said Henry.

But they soon forgot about Spence Morton as Norah and Mrs. McGregor joined them, with Pam close behind. They all enjoyed a cheerful dinner together. Even Pam was all smiles.

Benny was just polishing off his second helping of chocolate cake when he spotted someone waving. "I think someone's trying to get your attention, Norah." He nodded in the direction of a man seated a few tables away.

"You're right, Benny." Norah smiled and waved, too. "That's Bob Ferber. He did the work on my house."

A young man of about thirty came over. He had sandy-colored hair and a golden tan.

"Good to see you, Norah!" He put out his hand. "And you, too, Pam."

"How are you, Bob?" Norah responded, shaking hands. Then she introduced Mrs. McGregor and the Aldens.

"I'm afraid I ate too much," Bob confessed, after saying hello to everyone. "I seldom get a chance to enjoy such great cooking."

Norah smiled. "I hope business is going well," she said. "I know it's been quite a struggle to get it off the ground."

"Oh, it's not as bad as all that," said Bob. "I'll have my bills paid off soon—then it'll be smooth sailing."

Norah seemed surprised to hear this. "That'd be an amazing thing to do in such a short time."

Changing the subject, Bob turned to the Aldens. "So, are you enjoying your visit with Norah?"

Benny nodded. "We're solving a mystery," he said, his eyes shining.

"Oh?" Bob looked startled.

"At least, we're trying to solve one," added Henry.

Norah laughed a little. "I'll have to tell you about that mystery sometime, Bob."

"Right." Smiling uneasily, the young man glanced at his watch. "Well, now, just look at the time. Guess I'd better be off. Good luck with the old mystery, kids," he said, seeming eager to get away.

Jessie stared after him, puzzled. Nobody had mentioned it was an *old* mystery. How did he know?

* * * *

That night, after the Aldens had gone to bed, Violet lay awake thinking about Eton's Loop. What in the world was it? All day they'd kept their eyes peeled for clues. But

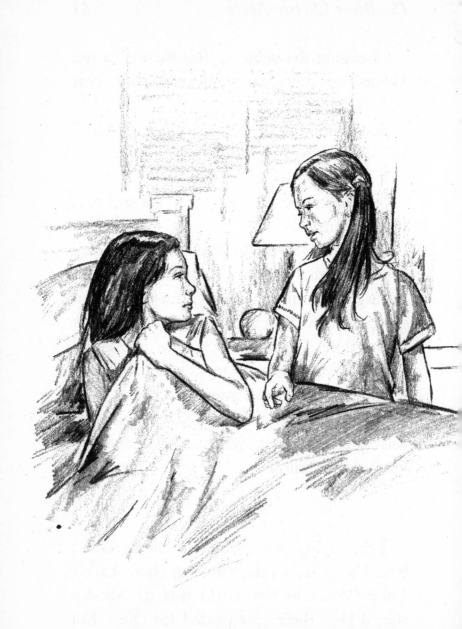

they'd found nothing that would help solve the mystery. Was the answer somewhere in the verse itself?

> *When last goes first,*
> *and first goes last,*
> *Eton's Loop will show you*
> *a clue from the past.*

Violet, who knew the verse by heart, was repeating the lines to herself when she suddenly heard something. What on earth was that noise? What could be—wait! She recognized that sound!

Violet slipped quickly out of bed. She gave her sister a shake. "Jessie," she whispered. "Jessie, wake up. Benny was right!"

Jessie sat up in bed. "What...?" Her voice was thick with sleep.

"I can hear water rushing over rocks!" Violet cried, rubbing her arms to take away the chill. "Listen."

Jessie sat very still for a moment. Then she said, "Your ears must be sharper than mine, Violet. I can't hear any—oh!"

Violet looked at her sister. "You can hear it, too, can't you?"

Jessie nodded her head slowly. For a moment, she was too astonished to speak. But she quickly pulled herself together. She was out of bed in a flash. She went over to the window and looked out. All she could see was inky darkness.

"Do you think it's true, Jessie?" asked Violet, who had just come up behind her. "Do you think that's the ghost of the Chattering Bones?"

"I don't know what to think," Jessie admitted in a hushed voice. "But one thing's for sure," she added. "Something very definitely odd is going on!"

Violet looked at Jessie. Jessie nodded back. They were remembering their promise to Benny. It was time to do some investigating.

As they stepped out into the hall, another door opened. It was Henry and Benny.

"You were right, Benny," said Violet. "We just heard it."

"It's the ghost of the Chattering Bones," Benny stated. "Henry heard it, too."

"I heard something," Henry corrected as

he led the way downstairs. "But that doesn't mean there's a ghost out there."

When they got to the kitchen, Henry reached for a long flashlight that was hanging on a hook by the back door. Then he turned to his little brother.

"Are you sure about this, Benny?" he asked. "Are you sure you want to go out there?"

"I'm sure," Benny said bravely.

With a nod, Henry opened the door and they filed outside. Closing the door behind them, they tiptoed down the creaky porch steps. Then, with the beam of the flashlight sweeping across the grass, they made their way closer to the bridge—and to the sound of rushing water. Then Benny suddenly stopped. He had seen something the others hadn't.

"There's somebody up there," he whispered.

Sure enough, a shadowy figure was moving across the bridge.

Henry beamed his flashlight upward. "Who's there?" he yelled.

As the Aldens gave chase, Benny suddenly

tripped and went sprawling. The others waited while he scrambled to his feet. But when they raced off again, it was too late.

Whoever had been on that bridge had escaped.

CHAPTER 6

Eton's Loop

"I don't understand it," said Henry as they had a late-night meeting in the room that Violet and Jessie shared. "Someone's going to a lot of trouble to make us think the bridge is haunted."

Violet frowned. "Who would do such a thing?"

"And how?" Benny demanded.

"Beats me," said Jessie, who was sitting on the bed next to Benny. "But it sure sounds like water's flowing under that bridge."

"Do you think anybody else heard it?" Benny wondered.

"Not likely," said Henry. "Norah and Mrs. McGregor have rooms facing the front of the house. So does Annette."

"What about Pam?" said Benny. "Her room faces the back."

Jessie shrugged. "Maybe she's a sound sleeper."

"Or maybe she has heard it," suggested Violet. "She does seem to think the bridge is haunted."

Henry said, "There's another possibility."

The others turned to him, puzzled.

"Maybe Pam's behind the whole thing."

"Oh, Henry!" cried Violet. "You don't really mean that, do you? You can't suspect Norah's niece."

"We have to consider everybody," said Henry.

"But why would she want to play a trick on us, Henry?" Violet couldn't believe Pam would do such a thing.

"You know, I've been thinking about Pam," said Jessie. "She said she never hiked as far as the woods. I wonder why she lied to us."

"That was weird," admitted Violet.

"What I can't figure out," said Henry, "is why Pam would lie about something like that."

"Or why she'd try to scare us," put in Benny.

"Maybe it's her idea of a joke," offered Jessie.

"Well, if it's a joke," said Henry, "it's not a very funny one."

"You know," said Violet, "There's somebody else we might want to include on our list of suspects."

"You're thinking of Spence Morton, right?" guessed Jessie.

Violet nodded. "Maybe he figures it's the only way to get Norah to sell her bridge."

"You mean, by convincing her it really is haunted?" asked Benny.

Violet nodded again. "He said he'd do whatever it takes."

Jessie looked thoughtful. "It's funny that he was sitting with Darlene last night. I didn't think he knew anyone in town. He said he was just passing through."

"Maybe they're working together," Henry suggested.

"You think Spence and Darlene are partners in crime?" asked Jessie.

"Could be," said Henry.

The others had to admit it was possible. After all, it was Darlene who first told them about the bridge being haunted.

"I thought of someone," Benny said. "Annette."

Violet looked puzzled. "Annette's a suspect?"

"She's trying to scare us away," said Benny. "And you know why? Because she wants to find the secret hiding place herself!"

That made sense to Henry. "You might be right, Benny," he said. "Annette's whole attitude changed as soon as Norah mentioned we'd be working on the mystery."

"And that would explain why she insists the brooch was stolen," Jessie realized. "She doesn't want anyone else looking for it."

Violet raised her eyebrows. "You think

Annette wants to steal the brooch?"

"Could be," Henry answered. "Don't forget, the brooch is made from valuable jewels. Maybe she needs money for school."

Violet still looked doubtful. "I know Annette isn't very friendly, but that doesn't make her a thief."

"No, but it does make her a suspect," Henry insisted.

"I don't think we should jump to any conclusions," said Violet, "until we have more evidence."

Jessie nodded. "We'll keep our suspicions to ourselves for now. Let's try to figure a few things out on our own first."

On one thing they were in complete agreement—there were a lot of strange things going on at Eton Place.

* * * *

After breakfast the next morning, Norah and Mrs. McGregor set off for town to do a bit of shopping. After waving goodbye, Henry, Jessie, Violet, and Benny went into the backyard to do some investigating. Maybe the person who had been on the bridge last night had left a clue.

"Let's spread out," Jessie suggested. "That way we can cover more ground."

"Good idea," said Henry. "If anybody sees anything, shout."

"Don't worry," Benny piped up. "I'll shout really loud."

After making a careful search of the bridge, Henry walked over to where Violet was combing the bushes. "Any luck?" he asked.

"Not so far," Violet admitted.

"We checked out the flowerbeds under the bridge," Jessie said when she and Benny joined them, "but—"

"We struck out," finished Benny.

"Hi there, kids!" It was Spence Morton. He was coming around the side of the house. "Is Norah around?" He flashed them a smile.

Henry said only, "I'm afraid not."

Benny folded his arms. "And for your information, the bridge isn't for sale."

Spence held up a hand. "Whoa, I didn't come to pester Norah. I'm here to apologize."

"Apologize?" Jessie echoed.

"I put a lot of pressure on Norah to sell me her bridge," Spence explained. "I shouldn't have done that."

"And you tried to scare everybody!" Benny said accusingly.

"What...?" Spence blinked.

Benny said, "You made it look like the bridge really was haunted."

"No, I didn't do that!" Spence looked startled. "I know I made a nuisance of myself, but I'd never pull a stunt like that." He looked at each of the Aldens in turn. "I have children of my own," he added. "I'd never try to scare kids like that."

The Aldens looked at each other. They had a feeling Spence Morton was telling the truth.

Spence continued, "Last night, I had a chat with the lady from the gas station. She told me that Norah's great-great-grandfather, Jon Eton, proposed to his wife on that bridge. She said he had it shipped all the way to America as a special gift for his homesick bride."

"That's right," said Violet.

"The article in the paper never mentioned anything about it," Spence went on. "I understand now why Norah refused to bargain. How can you put a price tag on family history?" He paused to gaze admiringly at the bridge. "Please say goodbye to Norah for me. It's time I was heading home." With a cheery wave, he walked away.

"Well, I guess that rules Spence Morton out as a suspect," Jessie said, climbing the porch steps.

"It rules Darlene out, too," added Henry as they trooped into the kitchen.

Benny sniffed the air. "Something sure smells good in here!"

Pam was taking a tray of cookies out of the oven. She smiled over at the youngest Alden. "Ready to do some decorating?" she asked him. "See what I've got? Butternut frosting and sprinkles!"

Benny didn't need to be asked twice.

After washing his hands, he set to work while Pam started on another batch of cookies.

The other Aldens sat around the table and tried to make sense of Meg's verse.

Jessie opened her notebook and read aloud.

> *When last goes first,*
> *and first goes last,*
> *Eton's Loop will show you*
> *a clue from the past.*

Once . . . twice . . . three times she read the verse. But it was no use. They still didn't have the faintest idea what it meant.

Violet glanced over to where Pam was adding a drop of vanilla to the cookie batter. "Do you bake at home, too, Pam?" she asked. "For your parents, I mean."

Pam looked at Violet in a strange way. "Why do you mention my parents?" she said in a cold voice.

Violet sensed she'd said the wrong thing. "I just meant . . . " her voice trailed off.

Jessie and Henry exchanged a glance. What's that all about? the look seemed to say. No one was sure what to say next. Then Pam dashed out of the room.

"That was odd," Jessie said, keeping her voice low.

Henry agreed. "Pam sure doesn't like talking about her parents."

"It does seem that way," admitted Violet.

As everyone gathered round to admire all the cookies, Benny said, "See the star-shaped one I decorated for Pam? Her name's on it."

Jessie tried to hide a smile when she saw where he was pointing. "You got the letters mixed up, Benny. You spelled MAP, not PAM."

The youngest Alden smacked his forehead with the palm of his hand. "Oops!"

"The letter M goes last, Benny," explained Violet. "And the letter P goes first." Benny scraped off the sprinkles and tried again. This time, he spelled Pam's name just right. Everyone cheered—everyone except Jessie, who wasn't paying attention. She had the weirdest feeling she was close to figuring out the puzzle, but she couldn't quite get hold of it. And then—in a flash—everything made sense.

"Of course!" she cried.

CHAPTER 7

Going . . . Going . . . Gone!

"Don't keep us in the dark," pleaded Violet. "What are you thinking?"

Jessie pointed to Pam's name spelled out in sprinkles. "See that?"

Henry nodded.

"Remember the first two lines of Meg's verse?"

"Sure," Benny told her. "We've read it about a hundred times."

Jessie went over to the table where she'd left her notebook. Pulling up a chair, she printed the words ETON'S LOOP on a blank page. With her pencil poised over her notebook, she recited, "When last goes first, and first goes last."

The others stared at her. They looked totally confused.

"I don't get it," Violet said as they sat down.

"That makes two of us," Benny said.

Henry added, "Three of us."

"I'll do the same thing Benny did," Jessie told them. "I'll switch the letters around."

She paused to look at everyone, hoping they'd see what she was driving at. "I'll make the first letter in each word go last, and the last letter go first." Jessie held up her notebook for the others to see—ETON'S LOOP had become STONE POOL!

"Oh, my goodness!" Violet said, putting her hands to her mouth.

"Wow!" said Henry. "That's good detective work, Jessie."

"I helped, too," put in Benny, who was busy scraping the last of the frosting from the bowl.

"You sure did." Jessie nodded. "You gave me the idea when you switched the letters around in Pam's name."

"What I can't understand," said Violet, "is what the village of Stone Pool has to do with the mystery."

"That's what we're going to find out," stated Henry.

Benny licked some frosting from a corner of his mouth. "How will we find out?" he wanted to know.

Henry thought about this. "Maybe the answer's in that photograph of Stone Pool. The one that Norah showed us."

Violet's eyebrows rose. "I hadn't thought of that."

"Let's keep a lid on this for now," Jessie suggested. "If it turns out we're on the wrong track, Norah's bound to be disappointed."

Just then, Annette poked her head into the kitchen, a pencil stuck behind her ear. "Hey, there!" she said, smiling as if glad to see them. "Do you mind if I join you?"

The children stared at Annette, wondering why she was suddenly so cheery and friendly.

Without waiting for an answer, Annette stepped into the kitchen, shutting the door behind her. "So . . . how are you making out with the old mystery?" she asked, giving them a big smile.

"Well, we figured out that . . ." Benny stopped talking in mid-sentence. He suddenly remembered not to talk about the mystery.

Annette was instantly curious. "Go on," she urged, as she pulled up a chair and set her coffee cup down on the table.

The children looked at one another. They didn't want to lie, but they also knew it was best not to discuss the mystery just yet.

"We have a lot of questions," said Jessie, "but not many answers."

Annette began to tap her pencil on the table. "Surely you've figured out a clue by now."

"A clue?" asked Jessie.

Annette sat back in her chair, looking at Jessie. Then, without another word, she got to her feet, grabbed her coffee cup, and marched out of the room.

When the door had closed behind her, the Aldens breathed a sigh of relief. "Can you believe it?" said Jessie. "One day she's making fun of us for being detectives, and the next she's—"

"Pumping us for information," finished Henry. "How weird is that?"

"Maybe we should forget about Annette for now," advised Violet. "We have a mystery to solve, remember?"

"You're right, Violet," said Jessie. "Time to check out the photograph of Stone Pool. I'm sure Norah won't mind."

"The album's in a cabinet somewhere in the living room," Benny recalled. "At least, that's where Pam was supposed to put it."

Sure enough, the Aldens found the album on the bottom shelf of an old pine cabinet with frosted glass doors. They made themselves comfortable on the sofa, then leafed through the album until they came to the old photograph. Jessie read the words at the bottom aloud one more time. "The village of Stone Pool as it appeared on a summer afternoon in 1810."

"That's funny," Violet said, looking over Jessie's shoulder. "The date's been underlined three times." She wasn't sure but she thought it might be some kind of clue.

But Jessie had a feeling the photograph itself contained a clue. She held it at arm's length, tilting her head to one side and then the other. "I don't get it," she said at last. "I can't spot anything unusual, can you?" She passed the photograph to Henry.

Henry bent over to examine it. "It's just a picture of a village in the olden days. Nothing strange about it." He passed the photograph to Benny.

"I can see lots of people going in and out of stores," observed Benny. "Nothing strange about that, either."

Violet took the photograph that Benny handed her and studied it closely. "There's something wrong here," she said. "But I can't figure out what it is."

"There must be something we're not seeing," said Jessie.

But Henry was having second thoughts. "Maybe we're on the wrong track."

Without taking her gaze off the photograph, Violet said, "I think we're on the right track, Henry. I've got a strong hunch about it."

"Well, right now we're going nowhere fast," Henry pointed out.

"And I think better on a full stomach," added Benny.

Henry grinned. "We get the hint, Benny. Let's get some lunch."

"We'd better not take the photograph into the kitchen with us," Jessie said. "We might get food on it."

As Jessie placed the photograph on the coffee table, she thought she heard something—a slight shuffling sound in the hall. Was it just her imagination? Or was someone listening to them?

* * * *

Violet swallowed a mouthful of soup. "It's so strange."

"What's strange, Violet?" Henry asked, helping himself to a grilled cheese sandwich.

"I can't put it into words, but there's something about that photograph of Stone Pool that bothers me."

"It's a really old photograph, Violet," Benny pointed out. "It's kind of faded."

"That's true, Benny." Violet poured more lemonade. "It's more than that, though. I can't quite put my finger on it, but something's not right."

"When it comes to mysteries," Jessie said, "your hunches are seldom wrong, Violet. We'll check it out again after lunch."

After the delicious cookies had been sampled, and the dishes done, the Aldens made a beeline for the living room.

"Where's the photograph of Stone Pool?" Benny demanded.

"It's gone!" Jessie said. "It ought to be right here on the coffee table."

Violet nodded. "I remember seeing you put it there."

"Then...what happened to it?" asked Henry, glancing around in bewilderment.

Violet had a thought. "Maybe somebody put it back in the album."

"I sure hope that's the explanation," said Jessie. She quickly checked it out, but it was no use. The photograph of Stone Pool wasn't there.

"I can't believe it," said Violet. "Who could have taken it?"

"A thief—that's who!" declared Benny. "And it looks like an inside job. I don't see any broken windows."

This made Henry smile a little. "Let's not jump to any conclusions, Sherlock."

"I bet Annette stole it," said Benny, who wasn't about to let go of his idea.

Jessie looked over at her little brother. "We shouldn't suspect people, Benny, until we're certain it was stolen."

With that, they walked slowly around the room, checking behind cushions and under chairs. But the photograph of Stone Pool had disappeared.

CHAPTER 8

What's Wrong with This Picture?

The moment Norah and Mrs. McGregor came through the door, Jessie told them about the missing photograph. "I'm so sorry, Norah," she said. "I know how much it meant to you. I just don't understand what happened."

"Oh, dear," said Mrs. McGregor, in a concerned voice. "First the tape recorder, and now the photograph. What more can happen?"

"Don't you worry," Norah said kindly, patting Jessie's arm. "It just so happens I made copies to give out to relatives."

"Oh!" The frown left Jessie's face.

"Besides," Norah added as she started up the stairs behind Mrs. McGregor, "it's bound to show up. After all, it has no value to anyone but the family."

The Aldens exchanged a look. Norah didn't realize the photograph could be an important piece of the puzzle. It had value to anyone who was after the brooch.

"There's at least a dozen copies in my desk drawer," she called down to them. "The den's at the end of the hall, kids. Go in and help yourself."

"Let's check it out," said Jessie, who was back to her usual cheery self.

With that, the four children headed along the hall. As they got closer to the den, they noticed the door was open a few inches. They heard a familiar voice.

"I'm telling you, it's a foolproof plan." This was Annette speaking. "Nobody suspects a thing."

The Aldens didn't like the sound of this. They knew it wasn't right to eavesdrop, but in this case, they felt they were doing it for a good cause.

"No...they won't be a problem anymore," Annette was saying. "What's that?...We'll leave no stone unturned?" She was laughing loudly now. "That's a good one!"

"Did you hear that?" Jessie asked the others, as they walked back along the hall.

Henry nodded. "It sounds like Annette's up to something."

"And she was asking about the mystery today, too," added Jessie. "That's kind of fishy, don't you think?"

"It was suspicious," admitted Violet.

Benny looked over at his brother and sisters. "Shouldn't we warn Norah?"

"It is a pretty strong case against Annette," admitted Violet. "But we can't be sure what she was talking about on the phone."

Henry agreed. "And Norah would never believe she was up to anything—not without hard evidence."

"You're right, Henry," Jessie said. "It's one thing to suspect someone. It's another thing to have proof."

* * * *

That evening, Norah, Mrs. McGregor, Pam, and the Aldens went to a baseball game and cheered for the hometown team. Even Pam couldn't help getting into the spirit of things. The game went into extra innings, and it was late by the time they finally returned to Eton Place.

After getting ready for bed, the Aldens got together for another late-night meeting. "I wonder who she was talking to on the phone," said Benny, still thinking about Annette.

Henry answered first. "Spence Morton comes to mind."

"You think Annette and Spence are working together, Henry?" Jessie asked in surprise.

"Could be," he said.

"Annette and Spence?" Benny repeated, not understanding. "But Spence left town, remember?"

"Maybe that's just what he wants us to believe," suggested Henry.

Violet thought about this for a moment,

then she nodded. "I guess it's possible he was trying to throw us off the track."

"Exactly," said Henry. "So nobody would suspect him."

Violet tucked her brown hair behind her ears. "Maybe it isn't the bridge he really wants."

"What do you mean, Violet?" Benny wondered.

"It's possible Spence is after Meg's brooch."

"Oh, I hadn't thought of that!" said Benny.

Just then, Jessie remembered something. She quickly told her sister and brothers about hearing someone in the hall outside the living room.

"Do you think somebody was spying on us?" Benny said.

Jessie had to admit it was possible.

"I wonder how much he—or she—overheard," said Violet, sounding a little uneasy.

"Enough to know the photograph was an important part of the mystery," Jessie responded.

The others nodded. No one would go to the trouble of stealing the photograph unless they knew it would help them find the brooch.

Henry had something to add. "Remember Annette saying on the phone, 'They won't be a problem anymore'?"

Benny nodded. So did Jessie and Violet.

"You think Annette was talking about us, Henry?" Violet asked.

"Yes," said Henry. "I have a hunch she was."

"I guess she thinks we can't solve the mystery without the photograph," added Jessie.

Henry nodded. "It's possible she took it without realizing there were copies."

"There's something I don't understand," Benny said thoughtfully. "Annette was the one who found the picture in the attic, right? If she wanted to steal it, why didn't she just take it then?"

"Maybe she didn't think it was important at the time," offered Violet.

"First thing tomorrow we'll get hold of one of the copies." Henry stretched and yawned. "Right now I'm too tired to think straight." With that, they decided to call it a day.

When Violet climbed into bed, her thoughts turned once again to the photograph of Stone Pool. She still had the nagging feeling that something was wrong. But what was it? She tucked the thought in the back of her mind as she drifted off to sleep.

* * * *

In the middle of the night, Violet cried out, "That's it!" She sat bolt upright in bed as the answer suddenly came to her. "That's why it was underlined three times!"

"Hmm . . . ?" Jessie looked over at her sister.

"I just figured out what's wrong with the photograph!" Violet threw back her covers and jumped out of bed. "Come on, Jessie. This can't wait until morning."

After rousing Henry and Benny, Jessie and Violet led the way down to the den. Sure enough, they found copies of the Stone Pool photograph tucked into Norah's desk drawer.

"So, what's going on, Violet?" Henry wanted to know.

"Think about this," Violet said, as they sat down on a little sofa. "The photograph's supposed to be from 1810. Right?"

Jessie, who was sitting in a circle of light from the lamp, glanced at the words in the old-fashioned script. "That's what it says."

"The problem is," Violet told them, "photography didn't come into use until the 1820s!"

Jessie blinked in surprise. "Then the photograph couldn't have been taken in 1810."

Violet nodded. "Meg got the date wrong."

"That's kind of weird." Benny wrinkled his forehead. "Do you think we found another clue?"

"I sure do!" Henry slapped Violet a high-five. So did Jessie and Benny.

"But...what does it mean?" put in Benny.

Nobody said anything for a while. They were all lost in thought. Finally Henry spoke up. "Are there any other mistakes?"

"I'm not sure," Violet said. "That was the only thing I noticed."

Bending over the photograph, Henry said 'hmmm' several times.

"What do you see?" Jessie asked, looking over his shoulder.

Henry didn't answer.

"Henry?" Jessie asked again.

"This is getting weirder and weirder." He ran his finger under the words in white ink. "It says the photograph was taken in the afternoon."

"What's weird about that, Henry?" asked Violet.

"The clock tower in the background says ten o'clock. The photograph couldn't have been taken in the afternoon. It was taken in the morning!"

"You're right, Henry," Violet cried.

"I just noticed something else." Jessie looked up from the photograph. "There's no way this picture was taken in the summer."

"What makes you say that, Jessie?" asked Violet.

"Look at the trees."

With their heads close together, the others took another look.

"No leaves!" Benny exclaimed in amazement. "The trees are bare."

"And there's smoke coming from the chimneys," added Henry. "Did you notice?"

Violet bent closer. "Now that you mention it . . . "

"Let's go over everything." Henry ticked off what they knew on one hand. "This picture wasn't taken in the afternoon. It wasn't in the summer. And it wasn't 1810."

The children looked at one another. How did Meg get so much wrong?

"I guess Jon Eton wasn't the only one who made mistakes," Benny pointed out.

"Jon Eton?" Henry gave his little brother a questioning look.

"He made a mistake about the bridge," Benny explained. "Remember?"

The Aldens suddenly stared at each other. "Jon's Blunder!" they all cried out in unison.

"I can't believe it!" said Violet. "Meg made all these mistakes on purpose. Her blunders were supposed to point the way to the bridge!"

"It all adds up," said Jessie. "Norah said the brooch disappeared around the time the men were working on the bridge. We're lucky Benny mentioned Jon's Blunder."

"Do you think . . . " Henry paused for a moment to sort out his thoughts. "Do you think Meg's brooch is hidden behind one of the stones?"

Jessie bit her lip. "If so, we have a big problem on our hands."

"What do you mean?" asked Henry.

"Remember what else Annette said on the phone?" Jessie looked around at them. "She said, 'We'll leave no stone unturned'."

Benny nodded. "And then she laughed."

Violet caught her breath in sudden understanding. "She knows!"

"Knows what?" Benny looked confused.

"Annette might have meant that the brooch could be hidden somewhere in Jon's Blunder," Henry informed his little brother.

Benny's jaw dropped. "Uh-oh."

"That would explain Spence's interest in the bridge," Violet realized.

Jessie said, "There's only one thing to do."

The others looked at her. "What's that, Jessie?" Benny said.

"Find the hiding place first!" she said.

"Well, what are we waiting for?" The youngest Alden was already heading for the door.

CHAPTER 9

Thief!

As they stepped outside, Henry was about to say something when Benny grabbed his arm. "What's that?"

Everyone turned to see where Benny was pointing. At the top of the bridge, a light flickered and vanished. There wasn't time to decide what to do. On the spur of the moment, Henry clicked off the flashlight and they made a dash for the nearby bushes.

The children crouched in the long grass, their eyes fixed on the shadowy figures standing in the middle of the bridge.

The muffled sounds of conversation reached their ears, but they were too far away to make out what was being said.

Benny whispered, "Maybe it's Annette and Spence! They might be looking for the secret hiding place."

Before anyone had a chance to comment, they heard a noise—it sounded as if someone were hacking away at the bridge!

"Oh, no!" Violet's eyes were huge.

Benny jumped up to peer over the bushes, but Jessie stopped him in time. "Stay down, Benny."

"But...somebody's tearing the bridge apart!" he cried, almost shouting. "What should we do?"

Henry said, "I don't know what's going on, but I think it's time to find out."

"Let's get closer," Jessie suggested. "Maybe we can hear what they're saying."

Keeping down, they crept cautiously forward. Then in a sudden burst of speed, they raced for another cluster of shrubs.

"Can't you work faster?" someone was saying. It was Annette!

"Give me a break!" came a grumbling male voice. It was clear the man was jabbing at the mortar that held the stones together. "I'm doing the best I can."

"The mortar's old and crumbling," Annette was saying. "Should be easy enough to get that stone out."

The Aldens looked at each other in alarm.

"I'm counting on your hunch being right," the man said. "Everything depends on it."

"I'm telling you, that plaque's the final clue," said Annette. "The hiding place is right behind that stone."

Jessie looked at Henry. It hadn't occurred to them before, but it made sense. After all, didn't the clues lead to Jon's Blunder? Wasn't that the name on the bronze plaque bolted to one of the stones?

All of a sudden, the battering noise stopped. "I think the stone's ready to come out," the man said. "Keep your fingers crossed."

"Thief!" Benny shouted. In a flash, he

had scooted out from behind the shrubbery. There was no stopping him.

The time for action had come. Henry and Benny raced onto the bridge from one side, Violet and Jessie from the other. Annette whirled around so suddenly, she dropped her flashlight. It rolled along the bridge.

"Who's there?" she shouted, blinded by Henry's flashlight.

"The Aldens," Jessie answered.

"I should've known!" Annette said. "This has nothing to do with you." She made a shooing motion with her hand.

Henry looked her straight in the eye. "We're not going anywhere." Then he shone the flashlight's beam on the man nearby.

The Aldens could hardly believe their eyes! It wasn't Spence Morton. It was Bob Ferber!

"You're the man from the potluck dinner," Violet said in surprise.

But Bob Ferber paid no attention to the Aldens. Instead, he plunged his hand into the dark space where the stone had been.

"Nothing!" He turned around, empty-handed. "Absolutely nothing."

Annette's jaw dropped. "How can that be?"

"You tell me!" Bob shot back. "You always seem to know so much."

"This is all your fault!" Now Annette was almost shouting. "You and your crazy ideas."

Just then, the bare bulb over the back door flicked on. Norah and Mrs. McGregor rushed out, pulling their robes around them. Half-walking and half-running, they hurried over to the bridge.

"Well, what's all the fuss . . . oh, my . . ." Norah stopped and stared at the gaping hole where the stone had been.

"What in heaven's name is going on?" Mrs. McGregor demanded.

"They're trying to steal Meg's brooch!" Benny said accusingly.

Norah looked from Annette to Bob and back again. "You two know each other?"

Bob struggled to find something to say. "Uh, well . . . I, er . . . " Suddenly, he stopped talking. His shoulders slumped and he leaned against the bridge, looking defeated. "Annette Tanning is my cousin." He could hardly look at Norah.

"What . . . ?" Norah was too shocked to speak.

For a moment, Norah and her assistant just looked at each other. Then Annette suddenly wheeled around to face Bob. "The whole thing was his idea," she shrieked, pointing a finger of blame.

Norah threw a sharp glance at Bob Ferber. "What do you have to say for yourself, Bob?"

Bob opened his mouth several times as if about to speak, then closed it again. Finally he let out a sigh and said, "All right, it's true. I was after your great-great-grand-mother's brooch."

Norah stared at him, open-mouthed.

"The truth is, I happened to come across an old letter," Bob confessed, "when I was working on your house, Norah. I guess it slipped through a crack in the floorboards a long time ago."

"Oh?" Norah raised an eyebrow.

"It was a letter from Meg Eton's grandmother." Bob hesitated a moment, then plunged in. "The letter made it clear that Meg was planning to find a safe hiding place for her family heirloom—a brooch made from valuable gems."

"No wonder you knew it was an old mystery," said Jessie, nodding.

Bob gave a little half-hearted smile. "I guess I gave myself away, didn't I?" Then he continued with his story. "I figured it was just the answer I was looking for. I knew, somehow or other, I had to get my hands on that brooch. The only problem was—" He stopped talking.

"You couldn't pull it off alone, right?" Henry said, urging him on.

"Right," said Bob.

Jessie guessed what was coming next. "You saw Norah's ad in the paper for a research assistant, didn't you?"

Bob didn't deny it. "It started me thinking," he said. "Annette was in the history program at college. If she got a job here, I'd have someone working on the inside.

It all seemed simple enough."

"I'm shocked at you, Bob." Norah looked grim. "How could you think of stealing from me?"

"I never meant to hurt you, Norah." He let out a weary sigh. "I was desperate. I ran out of money and I had bills piling up. My plan was to sell the brooch and make some quick cash. What could I do? My business was about to fold."

"That doesn't make it okay to steal," Mrs. McGregor said sternly.

"I know it was wrong, but I really couldn't see the harm." Bob shrugged a little, trying to make light of it. "After all, folks seemed to think the brooch had been stolen anyway. I figured nobody would be the wiser if I—"

"Really *did* steal it," finished Violet.

Bob nodded. "Turns out the joke's on me," he said with a hard laugh. "It seems the brooch *was* stolen—probably before Meg had a chance to hide it."

Norah shook her head sadly. "You're a bright young man, Bob," she said in a quiet voice. "Why steal? That's never the answer."

Bob didn't have a reply to that. He just walked away, his arms hanging limp at his sides.

Norah turned to her assistant. "You were really a part of this? I thought you were someone I could trust." She sounded more hurt than angry. "You tried to convince me the brooch was long gone. And all the time you wanted it for yourself."

Annette looked around. Everyone's eyes were fixed on her. "I've done a lot of things I'm not very proud of," she said, swallowing hard. "I actually wanted nothing to do with Bob's plan at first."

"But then you changed your mind," put in Jessie.

"I needed the cash. Besides, the research job sounded perfect. I figured I might as well try to find the brooch, too. Bob was going to split the money with me."

"That's why you were pumping us for information, wasn't it?" said Violet.

Annette nodded. "I had a hunch you might have figured out a clue."

"What about the photograph of Stone

Pool?" asked Henry. "Did you take that?"

Annette nodded again. "I was standing out in the hall and I heard you talking about the photo. I couldn't believe you'd pieced together so much. You're smarter than I thought," she added, looking around at them. "I was afraid you'd beat me to the hiding place."

"What you don't know," said Jessie, "is that Norah had already made copies of the photograph."

Annette looked surprised. "Well, I guess our plan wasn't really—"

Violet jumped in. "Foolproof?"

"Oh, you heard me on the phone, did you?" Annette sighed.

"Your plan almost worked," said Benny.

"Yes," said Annette. "Things were going nicely until you kids arrived. You don't give up, do you?"

"No," said Henry. "Not until we fit all the pieces of the puzzle together."

Jessie had a question. "There's one part of this mystery I still don't get," she said. "How did you make it sound like the

Chattering Bones was flowing under the bridge?"

Annette stared at Jessie, a blank look on her face. "I have no idea what you're talking about."

Norah had heard enough. "I won't be needing your services anymore, Annette," she told her. "Please pack your bags."

"I'm sorry I betrayed your trust, Norah," Annette said quietly. Then she hung her head and walked away.

CHAPTER 10

The Secret Hiding Place

"I just can't believe Bob and Annette would do such a thing," Norah was saying, as they sat around the kitchen table having a late-night snack.

"Some people!" exclaimed Mrs. McGregor, who was pouring milk for everyone.

Pam came over with a plate of cookies. She set them down on the table. As it turned out, she had alerted her great-aunt after hearing noises outside.

"I have a question," said Violet. "If it wasn't Spence who was trying to scare us

. . . and it wasn't Annette . . . then who was it?"

"It was me," Pam said in a small voice.

All eyes turned to her.

"You tried to scare us?" Violet asked in surprise.

"You're the one we were chasing the other night?" Jessie said at the same time.

Nodding, Pam sank down into a chair. "I . . . I'm really sorry."

"What on earth is this all about?" Norah looked at Pam in bewilderment.

Pam buried her head in her hands. "I thought my parents would come and get me if they heard about a ghost," she said, sniffling. Jessie quietly handed her some tissues.

"But how could . . . " Benny's eyebrows furrowed.

Pam lifted her head and looked at the youngest Alden. "You're wondering how I did it?"

Benny nodded. "It sounded just like water rushing over rocks."

"Wait a minute!" Henry snapped his fingers in sudden understanding. "You recorded the sound of the stream in the woods, didn't you? That's why we found your headband by the water."

Pam glanced sheepishly at her great-aunt. "I know it was wrong to take your tape recorder, Aunt Norah." Her voice wavered. "I'm really sorry."

Norah was too stunned to speak.

"You went outside in the middle of the night, didn't you?" Henry went on, watching Pam closely. "Then you played the tape back."

Pam didn't deny it. "I had it all planned before you got here." She could hardly look the Aldens in the eye. "But I hadn't counted on you being so nice."

"We were hoping we could be friends," Violet said quietly.

"You might not believe this," Pam said, looking sad, "but I'd already decided not to try to scare you anymore."

Norah hadn't said a word for a while. Now she spoke up. "I knew you were unhappy, Pam, but I had no idea why." She paused and sighed. "I still don't."

Pam twisted her hands in her lap. "I love

spending time with you, Aunt Norah, but . . . I miss my parents." Her face crumbled. "I just wish they wouldn't go away all summer."

"Have you ever told them how you feel?" Jessie asked.

Pam lowered her eyes, then shook her head.

"Maybe it's time you did." Norah put a hand gently on Pam's arm. "They're not mind-readers, you know. Why don't we give them a call first thing in the morning?"

"I like that idea," said Pam, giving her great-aunt a watery smile.

"I'm sure you're always in their thoughts," Mrs. McGregor added kindly. "And in their hearts."

Suddenly Violet's mouth dropped open and she almost spilled her milk. A wild idea was flitting through her head. "We have to go back!" she cried.

"Back...where?" asked Henry.

"Back to the bridge!" Violet was on her feet in a flash. She grabbed the flashlight and headed for the door.

Baffled, the others followed outside.

When they reached the middle of the bridge, Violet swept the flashlight beam back and forth. It finally came to rest on the stone with the shape of a heart in it.

"What's going on?" Henry asked, curiously.

Violet didn't answer right away. With a finger, she traced the name inside the heart—the name MEG.

"I don't get it," said Benny.

"When Mrs. McGregor said Pam was always in her parents' hearts, it suddenly hit me." Violet's eyes were shining. "Look at the name inside this heart."

Henry scratched behind his neck. "I'll not following you, Violet."

"Remember the first two lines of Meg's verse?" she said.

Everybody recited at the same time, "When last goes first, and first goes last."

Henry suddenly drew in his breath, catching on. "If you switch the letters around, then—"

"MEG becomes GEM!!" finished Jessie, her eyes wide.

"Oh, my!" said Norah. "Meg's brooch

was made from precious gems."

Henry said, "I think we just found the final clue."

"Wait right here," said Norah, heading for the house. She returned a moment later holding a screwdriver. "This is all I could find. But it should do the trick."

With that, Henry set to work. The mortar crumbled easily as he jabbed away at it. When the stone was finally loose, he put his hands on either side, then he wiggled and pulled with all his might. Slowly the stone came out, revealing a gaping hole.

When Violet shone the flashlight's beam into the opening, Benny couldn't stand the suspense. "Do you see anything, Violet?" he wanted to know.

"I'm afraid I can't—wait!" Violet said.

Everyone gasped when Violet removed a small rotted leather pouch from the hole. For a moment they all remained still, staring at the pouch. Then Violet held it out to Norah.

Untying the drawstring, Norah gently pulled out a small cloth bundle. Her eyes

widened as she unrolled the cloth to reveal a dazzling brooch. "Oh!" A broad smile spread across her face.

The Aldens let out a cheer. So did Pam.

"I've never seen anything like it!" exclaimed Mrs. McGregor.

"No wonder Meg wanted to keep it safe," Henry said.

Norah nodded. "But she didn't want it hidden away forever. So she left clues for her descendants to follow."

But something was still bothering Benny. "What about the Chattering Bones?" he said, puzzled. "Does it haunt the bridge? Or doesn't it?"

Norah put an arm around the youngest Alden. "Some questions can never be answered, Benny," she said. "There will always be mysteries."

"Well, guess what, Norah?" Benny said with a grin. "Mysteries just happen to be our—"

"Specialty!" everyone said together.

THE CREATURE IN OGOPOGO LAKE

created by
GERTRUDE CHANDLER WARNER

Illustrated by Robert Papp

ALBERT WHITMAN & Company
Morton Grove, Illinois

The Creature in Ogopogo Lake
created by Gertrude Chandler Warner;
illustrated by Robert Papp.

ISBN 13: 978-0-8075-1336-1 (hardcover)
ISBN 10: 0-8075-1336-9 (hardcover)
ISBN 13: 978-0-8075-1337-8 (paperback)
ISBN 10: 0-8075-1337-7 (paperback)

Cover art by Robert Papp.

For more information about Albert Whitman & Company,
visit our web site at www.albertwhitman.com.

Contents

CHAPTER   PAGE

1. A Monster Lurks   1
2. Hidden Treasure   10
3. A Sighting   24
4. Ogopogo Hunting   37
5. Strike One   48
6. Who Goes There?   56
7. Meow!   66
8. A Purr-fect Solution   76
9. Getting Warmer   84
10. Case Closed   100

THE CREATURE IN
OGOPOGO LAKE

CHAPTER 1

A Monster Lurks

"Do you think it's true?" asked six-year-old Benny. The youngest Alden had his nose pressed up against the window of their rental car. "Is there really a monster in Ogopogo Lake?" His eyes were huge.

"You mean, Okanagan Lake," corrected twelve-year-old Jessie, who often acted like a mother to her younger brother and sister. "Ogopogo is the name of the famous Canadian monster that lives in Okanagan Lake."

"I like *Ogopogo* Lake better," insisted Benny. "After all, it's the monster's home."

Henry, who was sitting up front beside Grandfather, smiled back at his little brother. "There's no real proof the monster exists, Benny." Henry was fourteen. He was the oldest of the Aldens.

Grandfather slowed down for a curve in the road. "They've even used underwater cameras to search for the creature," he said, "but nothing's turned up. Of course, that doesn't stop folks from keeping their eyes peeled. Everybody hopes to catch a glimpse of Ogopogo."

"Good thing I brought along my binoculars." Benny grinned.

"And I packed my camera," put in Violet, who was ten. Photography was one of Violet's hobbies. She almost always brought her camera along when they went on vacations.

James Alden and his four grandchildren— Henry, Jessie, Violet, and Benny—had just arrived for a holiday in the Okanagan Valley in British Columbia. They were on their way to the Ogopogo Resort in Peachland. Grandfather was renting a cabin from his good friend Abby Harmon.

"Should I check the map, Grandfather?" asked Jessie, who was the best map-reader in the family.

"That's okay, Jessie. I haven't forgotten how to get to Peachland."

"Oh, that's right," said Jessie. "You used to come here all the time. Didn't you, Grandfather?"

"We came every summer when I was growing up. My parents always rented a cabin from the Harmon family. Abby was about my age, and we soon became great friends."

"And you never lost touch," said Violet. "Right, Grandfather?"

"No, we didn't." Grandfather smiled at his youngest granddaughter through the rear view mirror. "We've been pen pals ever since. After Abby's father died," he went on, "she inherited the Ogopogo Resort. She still rents out cabins and runs a small gift shop."

"Sounds like fun," said Henry.

"Abby *does* enjoy it," said Grandfather. "But..."

"But what?" asked Violet.

"The place is getting old," Grandfather answered. "From what I hear, it's badly in need of repair. I'm afraid, with all the new resorts springing up everywhere, people aren't coming to stay at Abby's cabins."

Henry looked puzzled. "Why doesn't she just spruce the place up a bit?"

"Abby doesn't have the money for repairs, Henry. In fact, she's even been thinking of selling the resort."

"How sad!" Violet sighed.

"Abby hasn't made her mind up yet, Violet," Grandfather told her. "But someone said he would buy it. She's trying to decide what to do."

"That must be hard for Abby," Jessie said. "To make a decision like that, I mean."

Grandfather nodded. "The Ogopogo Resort is the only home she's ever known."

"We kept *our* old home," Benny said. "Thanks to you, Grandfather."

After their parents died, the four Alden children had run away. When they discovered an abandoned boxcar in the woods, they made it their home. Then their grandfather found them and brought them to live with him in his big white house in Greenfield. He even surprised his grandchildren by giving the boxcar a special place in the backyard. The Aldens often used the boxcar as a clubhouse.

They were all enjoying the car ride as they looked out the windows and saw the beautiful green orchards and vineyards. In the distance, dry brown hills were scattered with tall trees. Benny was the first to break the silence.

"I was just wondering," he said, sounding a bit uneasy. "What exactly does it look like?"

Grandfather seemed puzzled, but only for a moment. "Oh, you mean Ogopogo.

Well, it's supposed to be a long, snake-like creature with a head like a sheep. Some people say it's a plesiosaur."

Benny made a face. "A *what?*"

"A plesiosaur," said Grandfather. "A creature left over from the dinosaur era, Benny. It was thought to be extinct for more than one million years."

"Has Abby ever seen the leftover dinosaur?" Violet asked.

"Not that I know of," answered Grandfather. Then he chuckled. "Back when we were kids, we thought we'd spotted Ogopogo swimming in the lake. Turned out to be logs floating in the water."

"Ogopogo is a funny name for a monster," Jessie noted.

Henry nodded. "Not exactly a scary name, that's for sure."

"Ogopogo is supposed to be quite harmless," Grandfather informed them. "If there *is* a monster in the lake, it seems to keep pretty much to itself."

Benny looked relieved to hear this.

"I bet Ogopogo doesn't like being around strangers," guessed Violet. She was shy, and meeting new people often made her nervous.

As Grandfather slowed to a stop beside a fruit and vegetable market, Benny clapped his hands. "You read my mind, Grandfather!" he chirped. "I was just getting hungry."

"Benny, you're *always* hungry!" Henry teased. The youngest Alden was known for his appetite. They all got out and stretched their legs.

"I thought we'd stock up for the week," said Grandfather as they went inside. "The Okanagan Valley is famous for its fruit."

In no time at all, they were all busy filling their baskets. Jessie was checking out the cherries when she heard someone talking on a cell phone nearby.

"Of course, I'll do whatever it takes!" a woman was saying, sounding annoyed. "Look, I need this sale. I won't come in second. Not again. Not this year!"

Jessie didn't mean to eavesdrop. But from

where she was standing, it was impossible not to overhear.

"I know how to handle Abby." The woman was talking loudly now. "I'll get that rundown resort sold, if it's the last thing I do!" With that, the woman pocketed her cell phone and hurried away.

Violet couldn't help wondering if she'd heard right. Was that smartly dressed woman with the dangly earrings talking about *Abby Harmon?*

CHAPTER 2

Hidden Treasure

After making another stop for groceries, the Aldens were soon heading into Peachland. Everywhere they looked, tourists were strolling along the sidewalks and in and out of the shops and restaurants beside the sparkling blue lake.

"The resort's just up ahead," Grandfather told the children. "Keep your eyes peeled, everybody. If I remember right, there should be a sign hanging from a tree out front."

It wasn't long before sharp-eyed Benny

cried out, "There it is!" He pointed to a huge pine tree where three signs were hanging, hooked together, one on top of the other—OGOPOGO RESORT, CABINS FOR RENT, and OGOPOGO GIFT SHOP.

"Way to go, Benny!" said Jessie, as they turned into the gravel driveway. "Those signs aren't easy to spot from the road. The paint's all faded and peeling."

At the end of the driveway, Grandfather parked the car beside the long grass. Everyone piled out. Benny looked over at the line of cabins nestled among the pines.

"One, two, three, four, five, six," he counted. "Which cabin does Abby live in?"

"Abby lives over there." Grandfather nodded in the direction of a small building where a mustard-colored bench stood beneath a large plate-glass window. The sign above the door read: OGOPOGO GIFT SHOP.

Benny raised his eyebrows. "Abby lives in a *store?*"

"She has a small place in the back of the shop, Benny," Grandfather explained, as he led the way across a lawn covered with dandelions. "Let's go say hello."

As they stepped inside, a bell jingled above the door. A woman looked over as she tucked her short silver hair behind her ear. Her face broke into a smile as soon as she saw her old friend.

"James!" She rushed out from behind the counter. "It's been so long!"

"Much *too* long," said Grandfather, returning his friend's warm hug. "Abby, I want you to meet my grandchildren—Henry, Jessie, Violet, and Benny."

They all shook hands. "It's very nice to meet you," Jessie said politely, speaking for them all.

Benny glanced around. "You sure have lots of Ogopogo stuff in here."

Violet followed Benny's gaze. Everywhere she looked, she could see the famous monster on everything from posters to T-shirts.

Abby laughed. "That's our claim to fame

around here, Benny. Peachland is known as Ogopogo's home."

The four Alden children looked at each other in surprise. "Ogopogo lives in the town?" Benny asked in disbelief. "I thought he lived in the lake."

"Actually, he lives in an underwater cave just across the lake from town," Abby replied. "At least, that's what they say." She pulled a set of keys from her pocket. "I was just about to close up shop. Why don't I walk you over to your cabin?"

"Sure thing." Grandfather gave her a cheery smile.

"By the way," Abby said, "how does a picnic supper by the lake sound? I'm planning a get-together tonight."

Grandfather thought it sounded great. So did everyone else.

"I chose the cabin at the far end for you," said Abby. They followed a stone path that looped its way around the gift shop. "I've been airing it out, but...I'm afraid it still smells a bit musty in there."

Grandfather waved that away. "I'm sure it'll be just fine, Abby."

Benny, who had raced ahead, suddenly called out from the cabin porch. "Come and see this!" He sounded excited.

"What is it, Benny?" asked Henry, taking the steps two at a time.

The youngest Alden pointed to a large wooden carving of a green, snakelike creature with a head like a sheep.

"Wow!" Henry nodded approvingly. "That's pretty cool."

"There's an Ogopogo carving on every porch," said Abby, coming up behind them. "Patch O'Brien was quite an artist."

"Patch?" Benny said. "That's a funny name."

"His real name was Patrick O'Brien," Abby explained. "But Patch always suited him better." She paused for a moment. There was a faraway look in her eye. "I don't think I ever saw my old friend in anything but patched-up clothes."

"Oh, I get it." Benny nodded. "Patch was

his nickname because he wore patches."

"Yes—exactly," said Abby. "It's been a few years since he passed away," she added. "But I still miss him."

Violet didn't like to hear the note of sadness in Abby's voice. She was trying to think of something cheery to say when Jessie spoke up.

"It looks like Patch was an expert carver," she said.

"Oh, yes!" Abby's face brightened. "And you know, he made an especially wonderful carving of Ogopogo just for me. He left it to me in his will," she said, "along with his old boat, and—" She stopped herself in mid-sentence.

"And what, Abby?" Benny wanted to know.

Abby hesitated, then laughed a little. "Well, this is going to sound strange," she said, "but Patch also left me something rather odd."

The four Alden children were instantly curious. "What was it?"

"A riddle," said Abby. "It's supposed to lead to a treasure."

Henry blinked in surprise. "A *treasure?*"

"Wow!" Benny clapped his hands. "If you found a treasure, you could keep the resort!"

Abby smiled. "That's a nice thought, Benny," she said. "The problem is, Patch never owned anything of real value. Of course, I'd love to figure out the riddle," she quickly added. "But...I'm afraid I can't."

"Maybe we can help," Violet offered, and the others nodded.

"You never know," insisted Benny. "The treasure *might* be worth lots and lots of money!"

"My grandchildren are first-class detectives, Abby." Grandfather sounded proud.

"You're welcome to take a shot at it," Abby said, looking pleased. "I'll show you the riddle right after dinner if you like."

At that moment, a maroon car pulled into the driveway. A woman with reddish-brown hair, wearing a business suit, stepped out of the car. Jessie recognized her immediately. It was the woman she'd overheard on the phone at the fruit and vegetable market.

"Oh, that's Rilla Washburn." Abby waved her hand. "Rilla's a local real estate agent. And a good friend," she added.

"I thought you might enjoy these," said Rilla, rushing over with a basket of cherries.

After thanking her friend, Abby quickly introduced everyone.

Rilla gave the Aldens a brisk nod, then turned her attention back to Abby. "So...have you made a decision yet?" she asked in a businesslike voice. "About selling the resort, I mean."

Abby shook her head. "No, I'm afraid I haven't decided yet."

"You haven't decided?" Rilla did not look happy to hear this. "Listen, Abby," she said. "I don't mean to be pushy, but my client made you a very generous offer. If you keep dragging your feet like this, he might back out."

"I know." Abby sighed. "But this whole thing upsets me very much."

Grandfather turned to Rilla. "The resort's been in Abby's family for years," he pointed out. "It's not an easy decision to make."

Rilla frowned. "Well, isn't it lucky Abby has such good friends to look out for her," she said, but it sounded like she didn't think it was lucky at all.

Henry and Jessie looked at each other. Why was Rilla Washburn so unfriendly to them?

"It kills me the way you try to keep this place going, Abby," Rilla continued. "Don't you think it's time to move on?"

"Perhaps," Abby admitted. "But as James said, it's not an easy decision to make. I'm afraid your client will just have to wait."

Rilla looked as if she wanted to argue, but Benny spoke first.

"Don't worry, Abby," he said. "We'll find the treasure, then you can keep the resort."

"What?" Rilla turned around to face the youngest Alden.

"We're going to find a treasure!" Benny was all smiles. "The one Patch left for Abby."

Rilla threw her head back and laughed. "You must be kidding! Patch O'Brien never had a nickel to his name. Everybody knows that."

"But—" Benny began.

"No buts about it!" snapped Rilla. "Oh, I've heard those stories before—how Patch wasn't as poor as he let on. But you know what? That's about as crazy as believing in a lake monster. Absolute rubbish! That's all it is!" She turned to Abby. "Trust me, Abby. The sooner you decide to sell, the better."

"That's a very determined lady," Grandfather said, as Rilla walked away.

Abby unlocked the cabin door. "Yes, that's probably why she's such a good salesperson. You know, she's been runner-up for the top sales award seven years in a row. I'm keeping my fingers crossed she'll win this year. The award ceremony's just a few weeks away."

Inside, the Aldens found an old couch and some worn-out chairs grouped together around a crumbling stone fireplace. Tattered yellow curtains hung from the windows, and faded green wallpaper covered the walls.

Grandfather looked around. "Things haven't changed a bit."

Abby laughed. "That's just the problem, James."

"Well, I like it here!" said Benny.

Abby smiled warmly at the youngest Alden. "I wish everybody felt that way, Benny," she said. "I'd better go and let you get settled in. Now, don't forget about that picnic supper by the lake," she added, then hurried away.

The four Alden children began to unpack groceries while Grandfather napped on the couch.

"I really like Abby," said Violet.

"So do I." Jessie nodded, as she opened the refrigerator and put the lettuce away. "I sure hope we can find that treasure for her."

Benny passed a box of cornflakes to Henry. "Rilla Washburn doesn't think there *is* a treasure," he said with a frown.

"Well, it does seem odd," Henry had to admit. He put the cereal into the cupboard.

"How could Patch O'Brien have left Abby a treasure in his will if he was flat broke?"

"That's a good question, Henry," said Jessie. "Still, it's worth checking out."

"I hope Abby doesn't sell the resort before we have time to find the treasure," Benny said.

"Rilla sure was trying to get Abby to sell as soon as possible," said Violet. "I wonder why?"

"She's a real estate agent," Henry pointed out. "Whenever one of her clients buys or sells property, she makes money. That's how she earns her living."

"That's true, Henry," said Violet. "But she's also Abby's friend. Don't you think she should back off and give Abby a chance to make up her mind?"

"She won't back off until Abby sells the resort," said Jessie.

"What makes you so sure?" Violet asked in surprise.

Jessie quickly told them about the phone conversation she'd overheard at the fruit and vegetable market. "Rilla said she needs this sale, and that she doesn't want to come in second this year."

Henry nodded. "I bet she was talking about the top sales award."

"I have a hunch," Jessie said after a moment's thought, "that if Abby doesn't sell the resort, Rilla won't win."

"I think you're right," said Violet. "And she plans to do whatever it takes."

"Well, guess what?" said Benny. "We'll do whatever it takes, too—to find the treasure."

"For sure, Benny," said Henry.

CHAPTER 3

A Sighting

"See that boat over there?" Benny was standing by the water's edge. "The one at the end of the dock?"

The four Alden children were helping Abby get ready for the picnic. Henry looked over. "What about it, Benny?"

"I bet that's the one Abby was talking about," guessed Benny. "The one Patch left to her, I mean."

"You're right on the mark, Benny," Abby said, coming up behind them. She

24

was carrying a bowl filled with pasta salad. "That's the *Seven Seas*."

"What a great name for a boat!" said Jessie. She made room for Abby's salad among the plastic containers and covered dishes.

Abby nodded. "Patch spent most of his life sailing the seven seas searching for treasures. When he finally saved up enough to buy that old boat, he decided the *Seven Seas* was the perfect name for her."

"Was Patch a *pirate?*" Benny's eyes were wide.

"No, nothing like that, Benny." Abby couldn't help smiling. "When ships sailed the oceans long ago," she explained, "they were often caught in terrible storms. Sometimes the ships would sink to the bottom of the ocean. Patch was part of a diving crew that searched for lost treasures on sunken ships."

"How exciting!" said Violet.

"Wow," added Henry.

"Maybe that's what he left you, Abby,"

Benny exclaimed. "One of the treasures he found at sea!"

"That's not likely, Benny," Abby told him. "Patch had nothing but the clothes on his back when he arrived on my doorstep. I'm afraid he never got rich looking for treasures on the ocean floor."

Violet shook her head sadly. "That's a shame."

"Oh, not really, Violet," said Abby. "You see, Patch never placed any importance on money. He always said it was the search he enjoyed."

The Aldens understood. They were never happier than when they were on the trail of clues.

"Did Patch live around here?" Henry wondered.

"Yes, he made his home in one of the cabins," Abby told Henry. "He'd give me a hand with the chores in exchange for a roof over his head. Of course," she added, "I got the better end of that deal."

"Why do you say that, Abby?" asked Violet.

"Because Patch worked very hard. When he wasn't helping me, he was busy painting or carving. And let me tell you, everything he made sold like hotcakes. That's how he bought that old boat."

Just then, Grandfather came down the path, carrying a pitcher of lemonade. "Where do you want this, Abby?"

Abby laughed. "Wherever you can find room, James."

"Who else is coming, Abby?" Jessie asked. She had noticed the two extra places at the table.

"I invited Max Lowe and his son, Adam, to join us," said Abby. "They're staying in the second cabin down from yours."

"Will they be coming soon?" Benny asked hopefully.

"Don't worry, Benny." Jessie smiled at her little brother. "I'm sure we'll be eating before long."

Abby handed the youngest Alden a celery stick with cheese in it. "Here you go, Benny. This should tide you over."

"Hey, save some for us!" a voice called from the lakeside path.

Everyone turned to see a tall man with a tumble of sandy curls walking towards them. Beside him was a boy about Henry's age, his nose peeling from the sun.

"There's enough here to feed an army, Max," Abby said with a grin. Then she introduced the Aldens to Max Lowe and his son, Adam. "We've been talking about the *Seven Seas*," she told them, as everyone crowded around the long picnic table.

"Patch did a great job restoring that old boat," said Max, lifting some food onto his plate. "We sure make good use of it."

Abby nodded. "Max and Adam take folks out Ogopogo hunting," she explained. "Visitors get a tour of the lake and a chance to catch a glimpse of the famous monster."

"Sounds like fun," said Henry. Then he turned to Adam. "I bet you get all kinds of questions about the monster."

Adam nodded. "Everybody wants to know what Ogopogo looks like."

"We tell them as much as we can," added Max.

"They handle the boat tours for me," put in Abby. "In return, they get a free cabin for the summer."

"Adam and I really look forward to getting away from the city in the summer," Max explained.

Grandfather helped himself to the coleslaw. "Sounds like it works out for everyone."

"It sure does," said Adam.

Benny was wondering about something. "Adam, have you ever seen the monster?"

"Nope." Adam smiled at the Aldens. "We've been around the lake about a million times and we haven't spotted anything strange. I don't think there is a monster out there, Benny."

Max put down his fork and looked around at the Aldens. "Why don't we check it out? Who's up for some Ogopogo hunting?"

Henry, Jessie, Violet, and Benny waved their hands high in the air.

Max looked pleased. "How about meeting us at the end of the dock around ten tomorrow morning?"

"Sure," said Jessie. "If that's okay with you, Grandfather."

Grandfather nodded. "You can't pass up a chance like that."

"I'll bring my binoculars," said Benny. He sounded excited.

"And I won't forget about my camera," added Violet.

"Then it's settled." Max looked pleased. "It'll give us a good excuse to take the boat out. It's been a while since we've booked a tour."

"Yes, business has been pretty slow." Abby sighed. "What we need is a good Ogopogo sighting."

Grandfather chuckled. "I imagine that *would* bring the tourists into town."

"Oh, yes," said Abby. "Business always picks up after a report of a strange creature in the water."

"If I remember right," said Grandfather,

"Peachland holds the record for the most sightings. Doesn't it?"

"It sure does." Max reached for the pepper. "Every summer someone around here says they've seen Ogopogo."

"I bet I know why," piped up Benny. "I bet it's because Ogopogo makes his home right across the lake."

"You catch on fast, Benny." Abby smiled at the youngest Alden. "Would you pass the butter, Adam?"

Adam didn't answer. He was staring out at the lake.

"Adam?"

Adam still made no reply. When Abby reached out and put a hand gently on his arm, he suddenly jerked his head around. "Oh!" He seemed to have forgotten where he was.

"You're a million miles away, Adam," said Abby. "What are you thinking about?"

"I'm...um, not feeling very well," Adam said quickly. "Guess I got a bit too much sun today. Is it okay if I go back to the cabin?"

Adam looked over at his father expectantly.

"Go ahead," Max answered, a note of concern in his voice. "I won't be long."

Jessie couldn't help noticing that Adam had eaten every bit of food on his plate. Was he really not feeling well?

"I hope Adam's better by tomorrow," Benny said, as Adam hurried away. "For the Ogopogo hunt, I mean."

"I'm sure he'll be fine," said Max. "The truth is, Adam hasn't been himself lately. I'm afraid he's upset about the resort being sold."

Abby nodded her head sadly. "Believe me, the last thing I want to do is sell my home."

"What if you did some advertising, Abby?" Grandfather suggested. "It might bring in more business."

Henry, Jessie, Violet, and Benny all paid attention when their grandfather spoke. James Alden knew all there was to know about business.

"Yes," agreed Abby. "Advertising would help, James. But it takes money to advertise. And the truth is, I'm pinching pennies right now. Besides," she added, "it's awfully hard to compete with the fancier resorts. Some of them even have waterslides." She let out a long sigh. "Waterslides are very popular right now."

Violet spoke up. "What if we painted the signs out front for you, Abby?" she offered. "Bright colors would really make them stand out."

Grandfather nodded approvingly. "It would certainly catch a tourist's eye."

"That would be wonderful." Abby looked surprised—and pleased. "Are you sure you wouldn't mind?"

"It's fun to paint!" Benny piped up. And Henry and Jessie nodded.

"That's very kind of you," said Abby. "Now, there's a paint store in town, but it's closed tomorrow. Why don't you stop by the gift shop on Monday. I'll give you some money from the cash register, and you can get what you need. Oh!" Abby touched a hand to her mouth. "I almost forgot! I have something for you, Benny."

"For me?" Benny pointed to himself.

Abby reached into her straw bag and pulled out a stuffed Ogopogo. She held it out to the youngest Alden.

Benny was grinning from ear to ear. "Thank you very much!"

"Ogopogo will be good company for Stockings," Violet said, smiling over at her little brother. Stockings was a rag bear made from old socks. Violet and Jessie had made the rag bear for Benny when they were living in the boxcar.

Over dessert, Henry, Jessie, Violet, and Benny took turns telling Abby and Max all about their boxcar days. When they were finished, they gave Abby a hand clearing the picnic table.

After the dishes were finished, Abby led the way into her living room.

"Is that the carving Patch made for you, Abby?" Henry asked. He pointed to the Ogopogo carving beside the fireplace. The carving was attached to a wooden stand.

Abby nodded. "Yes, isn't it wonderful?"

she said with a smile. "Oh, speaking of Patch, why don't I show you that riddle?"

As they made themselves comfortable on the sofa, Abby reached for the photo album on the coffee table. She began flipping through the pages. "Here it is!" She handed a snapshot to Violet.

"Somebody sure likes cats," Violet said, as she studied the photograph of seven cats curled up along a weathered green bench.

"Patch had a real soft spot for them," said Abby. "He was always taking in strays."

"What happened to them?" Benny wanted to know. "After Patch died, I mean."

"Well, I couldn't take them in myself," Abby told him. "You see, they always made me sneeze up a storm. But I made sure they all went to good homes."

Violet passed the photograph to Henry. Henry passed it to Benny. Benny passed it to Jessie. They were each wondering the same thing. What did a snapshot have to do with the riddle?

"Flip it over, Jessie," Abby instructed.

On the back of the photograph, Jessie found a verse printed in black ink.

"What does that say?" Benny asked, checking it out over her shoulder. He was just learning to read.

Jessie read the riddle aloud:

> *An awesome treasure*
> *you can find*
> *with the clue*
> *I've left behind.*

"Wow," said Benny. "That's not much to go on."

"You got that right!" agreed Henry. "What clue did he leave behind?"

"I don't know! I haven't had any luck figuring it out," Abby told them.

"None at all?" asked Violet.

"Zero."

The Aldens looked at one another. How in the world were they going to find the answer to such a strange riddle?

CHAPTER 4

Ogopogo Hunting

It was dark by the time the Aldens headed back to their cabin. They were just climbing the porch steps when Benny stopped so suddenly that Violet almost bumped into him.

"I forgot Ogopogo!" he cried. "The one Abby gave me."

"Oh, you probably left it by the picnic table," guessed Jessie. "First thing in the morning, we'll—" But Benny was gone before she could finish.

Running full speed along the path, Benny made his way to the water's edge. Sure enough, his stuffed Ogopogo was right where he'd left it—on the bench beside the picnic table. He was just about to hurry back to his brother and sisters when he heard something—a splashing sound. For a long moment, he stood frozen to the spot, his heart pounding. Then, turning slowly, he looked out at the moonlit lake.

"Uh-oh!" The youngest Alden could hardly believe his eyes! In the water, not far from the dock, was the inky outline of a strange creature with three humps, a long neck, and a head like a sheep!

In a flash, Benny wheeled around and raced back along the path. He soon ran smack into Henry, Jessie, and Violet, who were on their way to find him.

Jessie could tell by her little brother's face that something had happened. "What's going on, Benny?" she asked in alarm. "Are you okay?"

Benny pointed to the lake. "Ogopogo!" he

gasped, trying to catch his breath.

Henry wasn't having any of that. "There's no monster out there, Benny," he said firmly.

Violet glanced over at Henry. She knew her older brother was probably right. But Benny's words still sent a chill through her.

"There's only one thing to do," Jessie said, putting a comforting arm around her little brother. "Let's go check it out."

Benny wasn't too sure about this. Still, he followed his brother and sisters back to the picnic table.

"Where did you see it, Benny?" Henry asked him.

"Over there." Benny pointed. "Close to the dock."

But when Henry, Jessie, and Violet looked out at the moonlit lake, they could see nothing but the old boat at the end of the dock. There was no sign of any monster.

"Whatever you saw, Benny," said Henry, "it's gone now."

"It was Ogopogo," Benny insisted, as they

headed back along the path. "I saw it with my own eyes."

"Remember what Grandfather told us, Benny?" Jessie reminded him. "When he was growing up, he was sure he'd spotted Ogopogo, too."

Henry nodded. "But it was just logs floating in the water."

"I'm sure that's all it was, Benny," said Violet. She wasn't really sure, but wanted her little brother to believe she was.

* * * *

The next morning at breakfast, the children decided not to say anything about Ogopogo, but they told their grandfather about the strange riddle. Jessie finished by saying, "Patch left a clue behind, but we don't know where."

Grandfather helped himself to a few strips of crispy bacon. Then he passed the platter to Benny. "It won't be long before you figure things out," he said with a chuckle.

Violet, who was spreading honey on her toast, looked up. "I hope you're right,

Grandfather. We have to find the treasure before Abby sells the resort."

Henry agreed. "We'll get started on it the minute we get back from the boat tour."

"Don't forget to wear your hats," Grandfather reminded them. "The sun can get pretty hot on Okanagan Lake."

"You mean, Ogopogo Lake!" Benny corrected.

Grandfather nodded and smiled.

"Don't worry, Grandfather," Jessie assured him. "We'll be careful."

After leaving the kitchen spic and span, the four Alden children said good-bye to their grandfather, then raced down to the dock. True to their word, Max and Adam were waiting for them by the boat.

"Glad you remembered your camera, Violet," Max told her. "It's a beautiful day for taking pictures."

As Max untied the boat from the rings on the dock, everyone put on their life jackets. Henry and Violet perched on the padded bench seat along one side of the boat. Jessie and Benny sat down across from them.

Max hopped aboard. "Ready to head out?"

Henry gave him the thumbs-up. "We're ready!"

Max started up the motor, sending the seagulls scattering. The *Seven Seas* was soon speeding across the water. For a while, no one said a word. They were all too busy enjoying the warm sun on their faces and the wind in their hair. Every now and again, passing boaters waved as they went by. The Aldens were quick to wave back.

When Jessie looked up, she noticed an airplane trailing a banner behind it. The banner read: FUN IN THE SUN AT THE OGOPOGO RESORT. With that kind of advertising, Jessie realized, it was no wonder Abby's resort was overlooked.

"That's Rattlesnake Island over there," Max told them. "According to local legend, Ogopogo makes its home in an underwater cave somewhere between Rattlesnake Island and Squally Point. Native tribes once called the creature *N'ha-a-itk*, or 'lake demon.'"

Jessie spoke up. "How did it get the name Ogopogo?"

"Somebody wrote a song about the creature years ago," Max explained, "calling it Ogopogo. I guess the name just caught on."

"Grandfather thought he saw Ogopogo once," Benny said, peering through his binoculars. "But it was just logs."

"Just about anything can play tricks on the eye," Max told them. "Even waves from a passing boat or a school of fish. And, of course, there's always the occasional hoax."

Benny frowned. "Hoax?"

Henry explained, "A hoax is when somebody tries to fool people."

"That's right," said Max. "I'm afraid fake Ogopogos crop up every now and again."

Benny said, "It's not nice to trick people."

"No, it isn't," agreed Violet.

Adam, who was sitting up front beside his father, said, "Still, it's possible Nessie's cousin *might* be living in the lake."

"Nessie's cousin?" Benny frowned again.

"That's the name of Scotland's famous

monster," Max explained. "Nessie's supposed to live in a lake called Loch Ness."

"Wow," said Benny. "You mean there's more than one leftover dinosaur?"

Adam shrugged. "Anything's possible."

Jessie looked at him in surprise. At dinner the night before, Adam had made it clear he didn't believe in the monster. Had he changed his mind?

"There's no proof that Nessie exists, Benny," said Henry. "And there's no proof that Ogopogo exists, either."

As Max turned the boat around, Adam looked back at Henry. "If Ogopogo doesn't exist, then why would the government give Ogopogo wildlife status?"

"Wildlife status?" Henry echoed in surprise.

Max nodded. "Ogopogo was given protected wildlife status in 1989. It's illegal to capture or harm it in any way."

Violet looked relieved. "I'm glad."

They were all lost in thought as they made their way back to the dock.

"Thank you so much for the tour," Jessie said, as they scrambled out of the boat. Henry, Violet, and Benny echoed her words.

"You're welcome aboard the *Seven Seas* anytime," Max told them. "I wish we could have stayed out longer, but I'm afraid Adam and I have some errands to run."

"No problem," said Henry, waving good-bye.

As they headed back up the path, Violet said, "How about a swim before lunch?" The others were quick to agree.

After splashing around in the lake for almost an hour, the Aldens went back to the cabin to make lunch.

"I have an idea," said Jessie. "Why don't we eat by the water?" She got out the cold cuts, bread, lettuce, and mustard.

"Sure!" said Benny, washing a handful of cherries under the tap. "I love picnics."

"Maybe we should invite Adam to join us," Violet suggested.

Benny shook his head. "Adam and Max are running errands. Remember?"

"Oh—right," said Violet.

"Speaking of Adam," said Jessie, "the way he was talking today, it sounded as if he believed the monster just might exist. But last night he said he didn't believe in it at all."

"Yeah, that was kind of weird, wasn't it?" said Henry.

"Maybe Adam saw Ogopogo, too." Benny's eyes were wide. "Last night, I mean."

"Maybe," said Jessie. "But I doubt it."

"I think we should concentrate on one mystery at a time," Violet suggested. "Let's work on finding that treasure before it's too late."

Nobody argued. They knew it would take all their detective skills to solve Patch O'Brien's riddle.

CHAPTER 5

Strike One

"Read it again, Jessie, okay?" said Benny.

Jessie pulled the photograph of Patch O'Brien's cats from her backpack. She read the riddle on the back aloud. *An awesome treasure, / you can find, / with the clue, / I've left behind.* The four Alden children were sitting cross-legged on a small raft tied to the dock.

Benny was puzzled. "How can we find the treasure," he said, "if we don't even know how to find the first clue?"

"It must be somewhere on the property," Violet said thoughtfully.

"But where?" Jessie passed around the napkins. "It'll take forever to search every inch of the resort."

"It isn't much to go on," said Benny. "Just a clue left behind...somewhere." He swallowed the last bite of his sandwich, then washed it down with lemonade.

Jessie looked at Benny in surprise. A funny look came over her face.

"Is anything wrong, Jessie?" asked Violet.

Jessie didn't answer. As she stared down at the riddle, an idea began to form in her mind. Then her face suddenly broke into a smile. "That's it!" she said, more to herself than anyone else.

"Jessie?" said Henry. "What's up?"

"The clue's right here!" Jessie told them, waving the photograph in the air. She sounded excited.

The others stared at Jessie. They looked totally confused.

"Patch left the clue *behind*," said Jessie,

hoping they would catch on. Seeing their puzzled faces, she added, "What's behind the riddle?"

Henry looked even more confused. "I'm not following you, Jessie."

"Wait a minute," said Violet. "Are you talking about the photograph of Patch O'Brien's cats?"

Nodding, Jessie flipped the riddle over. "I have a hunch the clue's hidden somewhere in this photograph."

"But...where?" asked Benny.

"I haven't the slightest idea," Jessie admitted. "But if we put our heads together, maybe we can figure it out."

They took turns studying the photograph—first Jessie, then Benny, then Violet, and finally Henry. On the second time around, Henry said, "That bench looks familiar."

"Really?" Jessie took a closer look. "I don't remember seeing a green bench around anywhere."

"Maybe it isn't green anymore. Take a

look at that crack along the back," said Violet, who had an artist's eye for detail. "It's just like the one on that yellow bench by the gift shop."

"You might be on to something," said Henry. "That's good detective work, Violet."

"Now we're getting somewhere!" put in Benny.

They quickly finished their lunch, then hurried over to the gift shop to take a closer look at the bench.

"No doubt about it," said Jessie, looking from the photograph to the bench and back again. "That's the same one, all right."

They weren't really sure what they were looking for, but they set to work checking out every inch of the old bench. They found the names of tourists carved into the wood, and wads of gum stuck under the seat. But they found nothing that would help them find Patch's treasure.

Finally, Violet let out a sigh. "Looks like we struck out."

As they headed back to their cabin, Jessie

said, "Never mind, Violet. It was a good try."

"If we're on the wrong track with the bench," Henry said thoughtfully, "that can mean only one thing."

"What's that, Henry?" asked Benny as he fell into step beside his brother.

"The clue must have something to do with the cats," Henry reasoned.

"That makes sense," Jessie said after a moment's thought. "After all, there's nothing else in the—"

Suddenly a familiar voice interrupted their conversation. When they looked over, they saw Max standing on his porch with his back to them. He was talking on a cell phone. The children couldn't help overhearing bits and pieces of the conversation.

"No, no! It's important to keep this hush-hush. I don't want Abby to find out what I'm up to...I'm not sure. Maybe gold."

The children looked at each other. They didn't like the sound of this.

When Max turned and saw the Aldens, he looked startled as if he'd been caught doing something he shouldn't. "Oh, hi there!" he said, quickly pocketing his cell phone. "I was just, um..." His voice trailed away. "Guess I'd better get back inside. Got something on the stove." He was gone in a flash.

"What was that all about?" Jessie said, with a puzzled frown.

"I'm not sure," said Henry. "But it sounds like Max is up to something."

"He was talking about gold," added Benny. "Do you think he's after Patch O'Brien's treasure, too?"

"We can't be sure what Max was talking about," Violet was quick to point out.

"That's true," said Henry. "I guess we shouldn't jump to any conclusions."

"One thing's for sure," said Benny. "Things are getting more and more mysterious!"

For the rest of the day, the Aldens puzzled over the photograph. But by the time they went to bed, they were still no closer to solving the mystery.

* * * *

Around midnight, Violet awakened from a dream about Ogopogo. When she couldn't get back to sleep, she slid out of bed. She made her way over to the window and peered out at the moonlit lake. Suddenly, she gasped.

"Jessie!" she cried. "Come quick."

"What is it?" Jessie asked in a sleepy voice.

"Hurry!" Violet cried. "You've got to see this!"

Curious, Jessie threw back her covers and jumped out of bed. "See what?" she asked, coming up behind her sister.

"Look over there," Violet said in a hushed voice. "By the dock."

"I can't see any—oh!"

Violet looked over at her sister. "You can see it, too, can't you?"

Jessie nodded her head slowly, too astonished to speak.

CHAPTER 6

Who Goes There?

"That's what I saw last night," Benny told them, his eyes wide with excitement. "It's Ogopogo, isn't it?"

Violet and Jessie had woken up Benny and Henry. Now they were all peering out of the bedroom window at the strange creature swimming by the dock.

"I'm not sure what it is," said Jessie.

Henry frowned. "It's kind of weird that a monster would be in the same spot two nights in a row."

"Do you think it's more than a coincidence?" asked Violet.

Henry nodded. "A lot more!"

"It does seem suspicious," said Jessie.

Henry headed for the door. "It's time to find out what's really out there on Okanagan Lake."

"*Ogopogo* Lake!" insisted Benny.

"We'll go with you, Henry," said Violet. Jessie and Benny were quick to agree.

Henry slipped quietly out of the room. So did everyone else. Henry grabbed a flashlight from the kitchen, then led the way outside. Everything was quiet and still. The only sound was the chirping of the crickets.

After tiptoeing quietly down the creaky porch steps, they hurried past the line of cabins. With the flashlight beam sweeping across the path, they headed single file down through the trees to the beach. The Aldens peered out at the dark lake. There wasn't a ripple. The strange creature had vanished.

Henry was about to say something when Benny grabbed his arm. The youngest Alden had seen something the others hadn't.

"There's somebody over there," he whispered, pointing.

Sure enough, a shadowy figure was standing near the boat.

As Henry beamed his flashlight towards the dock, Benny called out, "Who's there?"

Suddenly the figure was racing full-speed along the dock towards the water's edge. The Aldens gave chase, but it was too late. Whoever it was quickly disappeared into the trees.

They headed back to the cabin. "I don't understand it. Somebody's going to a lot of trouble to make us think there's a monster out there," said Henry.

The children had gathered in the room that Jessie and Violet were sharing. "Are you cold, Benny?" Jessie asked.

Benny, who was sitting beside Jessie on the quilted bed, was shivering. "You don't think there's *really* a monster out there? Do you?"

"No, that wasn't a monster, Benny." Henry sounded very sure.

"But how come it looked just like Ogopogo?" Benny asked as Jessie pulled a pine needle from his hair.

"I don't know how it's being done," Henry admitted. "But I'm certain it's a hoax."

Jessie agreed. "Somebody's trying to fool us."

"What I can't figure out," said Violet, perched on a trunk at the foot of the bed, "is why someone would want us to believe it was Ogopogo out there."

"I'm not sure, but I have a feeling Adam set it up," said Jessie. "This hoax, I mean."

Violet looked over at her sister. "Why would he do something like that?"

"I think I know what Jessie's getting at," said Henry. "A report of an Ogopogo sighting always brings the tourists into town, remember?"

Violet nodded her head in understanding. "You think he's hoping Abby won't sell the resort if business picks up?"

"Could be," said Jessie. "Max and Adam get a free cabin for the summer in exchange for giving boat tours. A new owner might not be willing to go along with that."

"His whole attitude changed," Jessie went on, "right after Abby said they needed a good Ogopogo sighting. Did you notice?"

Benny nodded. "He said he wasn't feeling well and hurried away."

"Exactly," said Jessie. "And then on the boat ride, he was suddenly talking as if a monster really existed."

"You know, Adam isn't the only suspect," said Violet. "I think we should add Rilla Washburn to our list."

Benny looked confused. "But...Rilla *wants* Abby to sell. Doesn't she?"

"Yes," said Violet. "But that won't happen if we find the treasure."

"You think Rilla's trying to distract us?" asked Henry. "Is that what you mean, Violet?"

"It's possible," said Violet. "Maybe she figures we'll start hunting for Ogopogo and forget all about the treasure."

"But Rilla doesn't believe that Patch left a

treasure," Benny pointed out, looking even more confused.

"Maybe that's just what she wants *us* to believe," Henry said. He was leaning against the pine dresser, his arms folded. "Maybe she's afraid the treasure might be worth enough to save the resort."

Benny spoke up. "I know somebody we should put at the top of our list of suspects."

"You're thinking of Max, right?" guessed Jessie.

"I bet he's the one trying to distract us," Benny said, nodding. "He wants to beat us to the treasure."

Jessie had to admit Benny had a point. "Max did say something about gold when he was talking on the phone."

Violet frowned. "We want to be sure he was talking about the treasure." She liked Max and couldn't imagine him trying to take Abby's treasure from her.

"Oh, Max is up to something, all right," insisted Henry. "I'm just not sure it has anything to do with the treasure."

"But it's true, Henry," said Benny, who wasn't about to let go of his idea. "Max wants the treasure for himself."

"If we prove it, it's true, Benny," Jessie corrected. "Until then, it's just a theory."

Violet let out a sigh. "It's hard to know who to trust."

"I think we should watch them closely for a while," suggested Henry. "Max, Adam, and Rilla."

"But let's keep a lid on this for now," Jessie said with a yawn. "We'll try to figure out a few things on our own."

With that, they put the mystery out of their minds as they went back to bed and drifted off to sleep.

* * * *

The four Alden children were up bright and early the next morning. Remembering their promise to Abby to paint the signs, they headed off to town right after breakfast.

"What do you think of purple for the lettering on the signs?" Violet asked as they browsed around the paint store.

"Sounds good," said Jessie, who was looking at a color chart. "How about this one? It's called Lavender Mist."

"Plum Delight is really nice, too," put in Violet. Purple was her favorite color, and she almost always wore something purple or violet. "There are so many colors, it's hard to choose."

It took awhile, but the four Aldens finally decided on Lavender Mist, Goldenrod Yellow, and Dragonfly Blue.

"Is it lunchtime yet?" Benny asked as they stood at the check-out.

Henry looked at his watch. "Close enough," he said. "I noticed a diner on our way over here."

No sooner had they stepped outside than Rilla Washburn came round the corner. She was wearing a green dress and matching earrings. She seemed to be in a big hurry, but when she caught sight of the Aldens, she slowed down.

"Well, if it isn't the gold hunters," she said, "or have you thrown in the towel already?"

Henry shook his head. "We don't give up that easily."

Rilla's smile disappeared. "You're wasting your time," she said. "Look, I know what I'm talking about. There's no treasure. End of story."

"But we already figured out something," Benny piped up. "Jessie, show Rilla the photograph of Patch's cats in your backpack. There's a clue hidden in the photograph of—" Just then, he noticed Jessie's warning frown. He'd forgotten they weren't supposed to talk about the mystery.

Rilla caught the look. "Oh, come now," she said. "You can tell me about it. Your secret's safe with me."

"We have to go," said Jessie, pointing to her watch. "Sorry."

"You're getting Abby's hopes up for nothing with this little game of yours!" Rilla snapped at them.

This was too much for Jessie. "We're trying to help," she said, looking Rilla straight in the eye.

"Well, you're not!" Rilla shot back, getting more annoyed by the minute. "You're not helping one bit!" With that, she hurried off.

CHAPTER 7

Meow!

"Can you believe that?" Jessie said as they headed down the street. "Rilla acts like we're doing something wrong."

"She doesn't want us hunting for the treasure," Henry added as they stepped inside the diner. "That's for sure."

Violet nodded. "She's afraid Abby won't sell the resort if we find something valuable."

Jessie nodded. "And that means Rilla would be runner-up again for the top sales award."

As they settled into a booth, Benny said, "She was wondering if we gave up already. We never give up."

"Rilla sure doesn't know us very well." Henry smiled over at his little brother.

Jessie passed out the menus. "Did you notice that Rilla called us *gold* hunters?"

"Hey, Max was talking about gold when he was on the phone!" Benny realized.

"Could just be a coincidence," said Henry.

But Jessie wasn't so sure. Her mind was racing. "Unless—"

"Unless what, Jessie?" Henry questioned.

"Unless Max and Rilla are working together."

The others looked at Jessie in surprise. "You think it was Rilla on the other end of the line?" Violet asked.

"It's possible." Jessie nodded. "If Max finds the treasure first, he'll make some quick cash, and—"

"And Abby would have no choice but to sell the resort!" Henry finished his sister's sentence for her. "It would work out very well for both Rilla *and* Max," he added.

Benny folded his arms, "That means there's only one thing to do," he said in a very serious voice. "Find the treasure first!"

"You're right, Benny." Jessie pulled the photograph of Patch O'Brien's cats from her backpack. "But we won't find it until we figure out what this photograph is trying to tell us."

Just then, a young woman with a cheery smile came over to take their orders. "What'll it be, kids?"

Henry chose a ham sandwich and lemonade. Violet and Jessie both ordered grilled cheese sandwiches, coleslaw, and milk. Benny decided on chicken nuggets, fries, and a root-beer float.

Jessie couldn't help noticing that the waitress kept looking over at the photograph as she took their orders. Why was she so interested in a picture of seven cats curled up on a bench?

"That should do for starters," said Benny, closing the menu.

The other Aldens looked at each other and smiled. They could always count on their little brother to have a big appetite.

The waitress gave Benny a wink. "Our chocolate cream pie is a big favorite around here."

"Do we have enough money for dessert, Henry?" asked Benny.

"Are you sure you'll have enough room?" Henry smiled as he waited for his younger brother's answer, even though he knew what it would be.

"I always have room for dessert," said Benny, who had a sweet tooth.

At this, the waitress couldn't help laughing. She added chocolate cream pie to their order, then walked away.

As they waited for their food to arrive, the Aldens turned their attention to the photograph of Patch O'Brien's cats.

"Just what are those cats trying to tell us?" Henry wondered. He was still convinced they were some kind of clue.

Benny had an opinion. "I think I know

what they're saying. They're saying—
meow!"

They all burst out laughing at Benny's
joke. "I have a feeling there's more to it than
that, Sherlock," Henry said.

The four Aldens were quiet for a while as
they peered long and hard at the photograph. There were seven cats altogether, and
each one was different. One was black, one
was charcoal-gray. One was small and
honey-colored, one was big and brown. One
had white-tipped ears, one had a striped tail.
And there was one that was a big ball of
orange fur.

"I don't get it," Violet said at last. "Do
you?" She looked around at the others.

Benny shook his head. "I don't see anything that looks like a clue."

"I've drawn a blank, too," Henry admitted. "This is going to be a tough one to figure out."

Jessie agreed. "All we really know is that
Patch loved cats."

"He sure did."

The children turned to see the waitress standing over them, looking at the photograph.

"I couldn't help noticing," she said as she placed their food on the table. "Aren't those Patch O'Brien's cats?"

"Yes," Jessie said in surprise. "Did you know Patch O'Brien?"

"Everyone around here knew Patch," said the waitress. "Real outdoorsy type. He stopped by the diner every now and again." She laughed a little. "Always ordered a slab of apple pie and a cup of coffee. My name's Tory, by the way. Short for Victoria."

Jessie returned Tory's friendly smile. "I'm Jessie, and this is Violet, Henry, and Benny." She pointed to her sister and brothers in turn.

After saying hello, Tory went on, "When Patch died, I took in Chad and Coco." She pointed to the photograph. "Chad's the one with the white tips on his ears. And see the big brown one? That's Coco."

"Cute names for cats," said Jessie.

Tory nodded. "My sister adopted Custard and Charlie. Custard's the black one, and Charlie's the one with the striped tail. Now, the gray cat—that's Crumpet. The owner of the gas station took her in."

"Chad, Coco, Custard, Charlie, and Crumpet." Benny was counting on his fingers. "That makes five," he pointed out. "What about the other two?" The others were wondering the same thing.

Tory thought for a moment. "I believe the orange cat and that little honey-colored one both went to a family on the edge of town."

Benny had another question. "What were their names?" he asked. "The cats, I mean. Not the family."

"Hmm, now just what were their names?" Tory was tapping a pen thoughtfully against her chin when a young couple came into the diner. As she hurried off, she called back to the Aldens, "Don't worry, it'll come to me. It's on the tip of my tongue!"

Benny was just dipping his last french fry into ketchup when Tory came back. "Clem and Chelsey," she said, looking pleased with herself. "Clem was the orange cat, and Chelsey was the honey-colored one."

Violet giggled. She couldn't help it. "They all have names beginning with the letter *C*."

"We always thought it was strange." Tory chuckled. "But the names are fun to say all together—Clem, Chelsey, Custard, Charlie, Coco, Chad, and Crumpet."

"I wonder why Patch did that," said Jessie. "Gave all his cats names beginning with the letter *C*, I mean."

"Well, he always did like the sea," Tory said, her eyes twinkling.

Everyone laughed—except Benny.

"I don't get it," he said, as the waitress walked away.

"Tory was making a joke," Henry explained to his little brother. "Patch liked the kind of sea you go sailing on. Maybe that's why he liked the letter *C*."

"Oh," said Benny, who still wasn't sure what was so funny.

"Seven cats—all with names beginning

with the letter *C*," said Henry. He was deep in thought as he pushed the salt shaker around on the table.

Violet looked at him. "Do you think it means something, Henry?"

"I have the weirdest feeling that we're close to figuring something out." Henry paused for a moment to sort out his thoughts. "I just can't quite put my finger on what it is."

CHAPTER 8

A Purr-fect Solution

Back at the resort, the Alden children found their grandfather sitting on the cabin porch with Abby.

"How did you make out in town?" Grandfather asked.

"We got everything we'll need for the signs," said Henry, handing Abby the change. "Sandpaper, brushes, and paint."

Violet nodded. "Wait till you see the great colors we chose!"

"Well, those signs can use a bit of pizazz.

But are you sure you want to spend your time working?" asked Abby.

Grandfather laughed. "You don't know these children, Abby. There's nothing they like better than hard work."

"Well, then it's okay. Oh, by the way," said Abby, "any luck with the riddle?"

Jessie didn't want to lie, but she didn't want to get Abby's hopes up, either. "We're still working on it," she said.

"I wouldn't spend too much time on it if I were you," Abby advised. "I'm sure Rilla's right. There probably isn't any treasure at all."

But the Aldens weren't convinced Rilla was right. They had a strong hunch there *was* a treasure. And it was a treasure just waiting to be found.

After a swim in the lake and a game of horseshoes with Adam, they got to work on the signs. Sitting in the shade of an elm, they sanded the rough spots where the paint was chipped and peeling. Henry worked on the sign for THE OGOPOGO GIFT SHOP.

Jessie tackled CABINS FOR RENT. And Violet and Benny worked on THE OGO-POGO RESORT.

Jessie had just brought out a thermos of lemonade when she noticed something that made her frown. "That's odd," she said. "Didn't Patch carve an Ogopogo for every porch?"

"That's right." Henry said. "At least, that's what Abby said."

Violet asked, "What's odd about that?"

Jessie gestured toward the line of cabins. "Take a look at the porch on the far right."

They all followed Jessie's gaze. "Oh," said Violet. "I see what you mean, Jessie. No carving."

"Maybe Abby sold it," guessed Violet.

"Everything Patch made sold like hot-cakes. Remember?" said Henry.

"Still, it is kind of weird," insisted Jessie. "I'm sure that carving was on the porch when we arrived."

"You know what I think?" added Benny. "I think the number seven is a clue."

"What makes you say that, Benny?" Henry questioned.

"For one thing, Patch had seven cats," Benny explained. "And for another thing, cats have seven lives."

"Nine," Jessie corrected.

"What?"

"Cats have *nine* lives, Benny," Jessie told him. "At least, that's how the saying goes."

"Nine?" Benny scratched his head. "Are you sure?"

Nodding, Jessie smiled at her little brother.

"You know what, Benny?" said Henry. "I think you're on to something with the number seven. After all, there are seven cats with seven names that begin with the letter *C*."

Benny nodded. "Clem, Chelsey, Custard, Charlie, Coco, Chad, and Crumpet."

"Very good, Benny!" praised Jessie.

The youngest Alden beamed. "A detective always remembers stuff like that."

"You think it's some kind of clue, Henry?" Violet wondered.

"Got to be," said Henry. "I just can't shake the feeling those seven *C's* must mean something." Just then, he clapped a hand over his mouth, surprised by his own words.

"What are you thinking, Henry?" asked Jessie.

"I'm thinking we should check out Patch O'Brien's boat," answered Henry.

"Why do you say that, Henry?" Violet asked.

"Think about it." Henry looked around at his brother and sisters. "What's the name of Abby's boat?"

"The *Seven Seas*," Jessie said, puzzled. Then her face brightened as she suddenly caught on. "The seven cats all have names that start with a *C*—the seven *C's!*"

"The cats are pointing the way to the boat!" Benny let out a cheer. Solving clues was always fun.

"You think there's something hidden on the *Seven Seas*?" Voilet asked.

"Let's go find out." Henry scrambled to

his feet. "Max said we were welcome on the *Seven Seas* anytime. And there's no time like right now," he added.

Henry, Jessie, Violet, and Benny put on life jackets and hurried down to the lake. They wasted no time climbing aboard the *Seven Seas*. As they began to look around, Jessie spoke up.

"Remember," she said, "anything that looks unusual can be a clue."

The others gave Jessie the thumbs-up. They were determined to check out every inch of the boat. But it wasn't long before Benny found something.

"Come look!" he called out.

Henry, Jessie, and Benny hurried over.

Benny had removed the life jackets stowed in the compartment under the bench seat. He was staring down into the empty bin.

"What is it?" asked Henry.

"I think I just found a clue!" Benny sounded excited.

The others crowded around. Sure enough,

a message had been carved into the wood at the bottom of the storage bin.

"Benny, you're an awesome detective!" Jessie said proudly.

"I guess I am." Benny grinned from ear to ear. "But...what does it say?"

Jessie read the strange message aloud.

> *Backwards or forwards,*
> *from left or from right,*
> *it's always the same,*
> *by day or by night.*

"Patch sure made hard riddles," said Benny.

Jessie began to copy the riddle in her notebook. "I just hope we can figure this one out."

"What's the same backwards or forwards?" Benny said, after a moment's thought.

Nobody had any ideas. It seemed like the more they looked for answers, the more questions they had.

CHAPTER 9

Getting Warmer

"Abby told me about a family park nearby," Grandfather said over breakfast the next morning. "They have bumper boats and go-karts and miniature golfing. Anybody interested in checking it out?"

"That'd be great!" cried Benny, his eyes shining.

Henry agreed. "That's a super idea, Grandfather," he said, every bit as excited as his little brother. "Besides, we could use a break from detective work." The four Alden children had puzzled and puzzled over the latest riddle. But by the time they'd gone to bed, they still hadn't come up with any answers.

"I promised Abby I'd join her for a cup of coffee before we leave," said Grandfather, taking the blueberry muffins that Violet passed to him. "But it won't take long."

After breakfast, the four Alden children cleared the table and washed the dishes while Grandfather had coffee with Abby.

"Let's take your notebook with us, Jessie," suggested Violet, who was giving the counters a once-over. "We can try to figure out the riddle on the drive."

"I was thinking the same thing," Henry agreed. "We really don't have time to take a break from this mystery."

"I put the notebook in my backpack," said Jessie, glancing around the room. "Now...where did I leave the backpack?"

Violet looked around, too. "Maybe it's outside. The last time I remember seeing it was when we were painting the signs."

Benny was already halfway to the door. "I bet we left it by that big tree."

The Aldens wasted no time checking it out. Sure enough, Jessie's denim backpack was leaning up against the trunk of the old elm tree.

"It's right where we left—oh, no!" Benny exclaimed.

"What in the world…?" Violet cried out at the same time.

The four Aldens stared in astonishment. The words MIND YOUR OWN BUSINESS—OR ELSE! had been painted in purple across one of the signboards.

Henry gave a low whistle. "Somebody sure doesn't want us looking for that treasure."

Benny's eyes were huge. "Who do you think…?"

"Could be anybody," Jessie broke in as she fished through the denim backpack for her notebook.

Henry used a stick to pry open the lid on the can of Goldenrod Yellow. "It'll take more than a message in purple to get us to back off," he said. Then he grabbed a paint brush and slapped a thick coat of Goldenrod Yellow over the words.

"It's gone!" Jessie suddenly cried out.

Henry looked up. "What's gone?"

"Are you talking about your notebook, Jessie?" Violet wanted to know.

Jessie shook her head. "My notebook is here, but...the photograph is gone!"

"Are you positive you left it in your backpack?" Henry wanted to make sure.

"Yes," said Jessie. "It was right in this zippered pocket with the notebook."

"I don't understand." Violet frowned. "It couldn't just disappear."

"It could if somebody stole it," Benny said. "And I bet it was the same person who left that message."

"Oh, Benny!" Violet exclaimed. "Why would anyone steal an old photograph of cats?"

"Unless," Jessie remarked, "he—or she— knew the photo held a clue to the treasure."

"Uh-oh," said Benny.

Henry looked over at his little brother. "What is it, Benny?"

"Rilla Washburn knew about the clue," Benny said in a quiet voice. "I gave away top-secret information when we saw her in town. Remember?"

"That's okay, Benny," Jessie assured him. "At least the thief didn't take my notebook."

The children forgot all about the mystery for a while when they got to the amusement park. They rode the bumper boats and the go-karts and did some wall climbing. Even Grandfather joined them for a game of miniature golf. Everyone had a wonderful time—at least until they were heading back to the resort. When they stopped at a café for lunch, Grandfather told them the news.

"It seems Abby's made up her mind," he said after the waitress had brought their food. They'd all ordered the special—cold turkey sandwiches, homemade potato chips, and root beer. "She's decided to sell the Ogopogo Resort."

"What...?" Benny almost choked on a potato chip.

"Oh, no!" Violet cried at the same time.

"I'm afraid it's true," said Grandfather. As he took a sip of root beer, the ice cubes clinked in the glass. "She told me this morning."

The four Aldens looked at each other in dismay. They'd been so sure they'd find the treasure in time!

Grandfather swallowed a bite of his sandwich. "She's planning to put in a call to her real estate agent today."

"*Today?*" Henry winced.

"Abby's made up her mind," said Grandfather. "I told her I'd look over the sales contract with her. It's important to check out the small print."

Benny frowned. "But we were getting warmer."

Grandfather smiled at his youngest grandson. "I know you were hoping to save the day, Benny," he said. "But things don't always work out the way we plan."

Violet let out a sigh. "I just wish things weren't working out the way Rilla planned."

"Abby hasn't sold the resort yet, Violet," Jessie reminded her, before crunching into a potato chip.

"That's true," said Henry. "And we haven't given up yet, have we?"

"No!" the other Aldens almost shouted.

True to their word, the moment they got back to the resort, the four children turned their attention once again to the latest riddle.

To refresh their memories, Jessie pulled out her notebook and began to recite, *Backwards or forwards, / from left or from right, / it's always the same, / by day or by night.*

Nobody said anything. They were deep in thought as they continued to paint signs.

"I still don't get it," Benny said, dipping his brush into the can of Lavender Mist. "What's the same backwards or forwards?"

Violet couldn't help laughing when she looked over at her little brother. "Oh, Benny!" she said. "You look like you've been face-painting."

The youngest Alden had a smear of Goldenrod Yellow on his chin, a drop of Dragonfly Blue on the tip of his nose, and a splattering of Lavender Mist on his forehead.

"Paint likes my face," said Benny, making them all laugh.

"I think paint likes your clothes, too," Henry joked, making them laugh even harder.

Just then, they heard the crunch of tires on gravel. They looked over to see Max getting out of his car. Smiling, he came across the grass, carrying a package under his arm.

"Great job!" He looked down at the signs approvingly. "They'll be real easy to spot now."

Benny gave him a half-hearted smile. "It won't really matter."

"Yeah, I heard the news." Max stopped smiling. "I kept hoping Abby wouldn't sell, but..." His words trailed away.

"We were all hoping Abby wouldn't sell," put in Jessie.

"Listen," said Max. He lowered his voice as if about to share a secret. "I could use your opinion on something." Taking the package from under his arm, he tore away the wrapping. "What do you think?" he asked, holding up a painting in a wood frame.

"That's a picture of this place," Benny realized. "And you can even see Ogopogo Lake in the background."

Max looked puzzled. "Ogopogo Lake?"

"That's what Benny calls Okanagan Lake," Jessie explained.

"It's a beautiful painting," said Violet, taking a closer look. The watercolor showed a row of cabins nestled amongst the trees, with a lake in the background. "Oh—look at the bottom corner!"

"That's Patch O'Brien's signature." Max was beaming.

Henry gave Max a questioning look. "Abby's friend painted that?"

Max nodded. "I found it in our cabin— shoved in the back of a closet," he said. "I got it framed to surprise Abby."

"She'll love it," Jessie said, and the others nodded.

"You think the frame's okay, then?" Max wanted to know.

Violet said, "That dark wood is perfect for the painting."

"I thought so, too," said Max, looking relieved. "At first, I thought a gold frame would be best. But then, on a hunch, I went with the dark wood."

The Aldens exchanged glances. A *gold* frame? That must have been the phone conversation they'd overheard.

"I'll give it to Abby tonight," Max went on, "after Rilla Washburn leaves. I'm hoping this little surprise will cheer her up a bit."

Violet nodded in sudden understanding. That's what Max had meant about keeping things hush-hush. He had wanted the painting to be a surprise.

"Our lips are sealed," Henry promised.

"Looks like that's one suspect we can cross off our list," Jessie said when Max was out of earshot.

Nodding, Violet smiled a little. She knew Max could never be Rilla's partner in crime.

"I'm almost finished here," Henry said, dabbing his brush into Dragonfly Blue paint.

"Me, too," said Jessie.

"Violet and I just have the letters for OGO-POGO left," Benny put in. "We already did RESORT."

"How about this, Benny?" said Violet. "I'll paint the letters O—G—O at the beginning, and you paint the letters O—G—O at the end."

"Sure," Benny agreed. "And we can both do the letter P in the middle."

Violet couldn't help laughing. "Did you notice? OGOPOGO is spelled the same both ways."

Benny took another look. "Hey, you're right, Violet!" he said in surprise. "That's kind of funny, isn't it?"

"It's called a palindrome," said Jessie.

"A palin-what?" Benny asked.

"Palindrome," Jessie repeated. "That's a word that's spelled the same backwards or—"

"Forwards!" finished Henry, snapping his fingers. He sounded excited.

Violet and Benny looked over at their older brother and sister, puzzled.

"Remember the riddle?" Jessie explained, slapping Henry a high-five. *"Backwards or forwards, / from left or from right, / it's always the same, / by day or by night."*

"Wait a minute," cried Benny. *"Ogopogo* is the answer to the riddle? Is that what you mean, Jessie?"

Jessie nodded. "That's exactly what I mean, Benny."

"Yeah!" shouted the youngest Alden. So did the others.

"But what does Ogopogo have to do with the treasure?" Violet wondered.

Benny's face lit up. "I bet the treasure's hidden in one of Ogopogo's underwater caves!"

"Could be," said Henry. "But I have a feeling it's closer than that."

"Do you think it's on the property some-where, Henry?" Violet wanted to know.

Henry didn't seem to hear the question. He was busy fishing around in the can of purple paint. "That's weird," he said. "There's something floating in here."

Curious, the other Aldens moved closer. Henry removed a small object from the can. It was dripping with paint.

"What is that?" Benny wanted to know.

"I'm not sure." Henry reached for a rag to wipe away the paint. "Looks like jewelry."

"What's jewelry doing in a can of purple paint?" Benny asked as Henry held up a long, dangly earring.

"Wait a minute," said Violet, leaning in closer. "Are those green stones?"

Henry grabbed the rag and gave the earring another once-over. "Yeah, the stones are definitely green."

Jessie turned to her younger sister. "What are you thinking, Violet?"

"It looks familiar," Violet said. "I've seen that earring somewhere before."

Just then, another car pulled into the driveway. They watched as Rilla

Washburn climbed out and made a beeline for the gift shop.

"Of course!" Violet cried. "Rilla was wearing the same earrings. When we ran into her in town, I mean."

"Are you sure about that, Violet?" Henry asked.

Violet nodded her head up and down. "I remember how well the stones matched her dress."

"But…how did Rilla's earring get into the paint?" Benny wanted to know.

Henry had an answer. "It probably fell in when she was leaving that message."

"Right before she stole the picture of Patch's cats out of Jessie's backpack," added Violet.

"You think Rilla is the person who left the message telling us to mind our own business—or else, *and* stole the picture?" asked Jessie.

"It had to be her," Henry insisted. "How else can you explain her earring getting into the paint?"

"Shouldn't we tell Abby?" Benny wondered.

"The problem is," Jessie told her little brother. "we can't *prove* the earring belongs to Rilla."

"And she'd never admit it was hers," added Violet. "Otherwise, she'd have to explain how it got into the paint."

"Maybe she doesn't even know that's what happened," Henry said. "Let's tell her we found her earring and see what happens."

CHAPTER 10

Case Closed

The children could hear voices in the living room. "Something's come up," Henry said as they went in.

"What is it, Henry?" asked Grandfather. He was sitting on the couch, with Rilla Washburn perched in a chair nearby. "Is anything wrong?"

Henry shook his head. "No, but—"

"Well, if nothing's wrong," Rilla cut in sharply, "I suggest you come back later. We're trying to have a business meeting here."

"We're sorry to interrupt," said Jessie, who was always polite. "We'll be out of your way in a minute."

Henry held the earring out to Rilla in the palm of his hand. "We thought this might be yours."

"Oh!" Rilla's face perked up. "I've been looking everywhere for that." She snatched the earring from Henry's hand. "Where did you find it?"

"In a can of paint," Henry answered, watching her closely.

"What...?" A funny look came over Rilla's face. "Why, I can't imagine how—"

Henry cut in, "Maybe it fell in when you were leaving that message for us."

"On one of Abby's signboards," added Benny, his hands on his hips.

"A message on a signboard?" Rilla lifted her hands as if she was confused. "I'm afraid I don't know what you're talking about."

"It was a message telling us to mind our own business," Jessie reminded her, "or else!"

"Oh, my goodness!" A look of shock crossed Abby's face. "What is this about?"

"You think I'd do such a thing, Abby?" Rilla looked hurt. "I have no idea what these kids are up to," she added, "but you can be sure they didn't find this earring in a can of purple paint!"

"Nobody said it was *purple* paint," Violet said quietly. "How did you know that?"

"Uh, well...I, er..." Rilla struggled to find something to say.

"Rilla!" Abby cried. "Is this true? Did you leave a threatening message for these children?"

Rilla opened her mouth, then closed it again. Finally, she slumped back against the cushions. "Yes, I did leave that message, and I feel terrible about it." She lowered her head and sniffed, pretending to cry.

Abby was so startled, she needed a few moments to collect her thoughts. "But...why?"

"That's just what I was wondering," Grandfather said sternly.

Rilla looked up and gave a little smile.

"It's really not such a big deal, is it?"

"You wanted us to stop looking for the treasure, didn't you?" guessed Violet.

Rilla didn't deny it. "Treasure-hunting does sound harmless," she said. "But I knew it would cause problems later on."

"Problems?" Abby looked even more confused. "What kind of problems?"

Jessie spoke up. "If we found the treasure, there'd be no reason for you to sell the resort, Abby."

"And if you didn't sell the resort to Rilla, then she would miss out on the top sales award *again*," added Henry.

"That's why Rilla was trying to scare us by leaving us that message, and why she stole the picture Patch left Abby with the riddle leading to the treasure," added Violet.

"What?" Rilla exclaimed. "I did nothing of the sort!" Rilla began to defend herself and then quickly gave up as she saw that everyone in the room knew what she had done.

"Fine," she said. "When Benny mentioned Jessie had a photo in her backpack with a clue to the treasure written on it, I decided to take it." Rilla reached into her purse, pulled out the old snapshot, and handed it to Abby. "I couldn't let anything get in the way of this sale! I've missed out on the top sales award too many times, and if I sold this resort, nothing could stop me from winning," Rilla explained.

Abby looked hurt. "You know how much this resort means to me, Rilla. I would have hoped our friendship was more important to you than the top sales award."

Rilla sat quietly.

"And that's not all," Benny chimed in. "Rilla even made a fake monster to scare us away!"

"No, I didn't do any such thing!" Rilla's dark eyes suddenly flashed. "I don't know anything about a fake monster."

The Aldens looked at each other. They had a feeling Rilla was telling the truth.

"I did leave that message and I stole the

picture, but that's all," she went on. "I'm so sorry, Abby. I never meant for this to go so far."

"Sorry isn't enough," said Abby. "I draw the line at leaving threatening messages for children."

"You're right, Abby. I did get carried away," said Rilla. "But the resort still needs to be sold. My client made you a good offer."

Abby got to her feet. "I'll have to pass."

Rilla waved away Abby's words. "Now, none of that. We can't let friendship get in the way of business, can we?" she said. "Or business get in the way of friendship, for that matter."

Abby had heard enough. "You and I have different ideas about friendship, Rilla. I'm afraid I must ask you to leave."

"You can't mean it!"

"Yes, I do, Rilla." Abby folded her arms, a no-nonsense look on her face.

"Fine!" Rilla headed for the door. As she left, she called back, "You won't be seeing me around here again!"

"I'm counting on it," replied Abby.

As the door slammed shut, Grandfather said, "I guess that's that."

"Actually, it's a load off my mind, James." Abby sat down again. "I really wasn't ready to sell the resort. Not just yet, anyway."

"Is the coast clear?" asked Max, sticking his head into the room.

Nodding, Abby gestured for him to come in. "Rilla's gone."

Max stepped into the room, the painting tucked under his arm. Adam was close behind.

"It didn't take you long to close the deal, Abby," Max remarked, pulling up a chair.

"I decided not to sell the resort, Max."

Max and Adam stared at Abby in surprise. "You mean, you still own the Ogopogo Resort?" Adam wanted to know.

"For the moment, at least." Abby quickly explained what had happened. She finished by saying, "When I do sell the resort, it won't be with Rilla Washburn's agency. You can be sure of that."

"Well, Adam and I brought you a present," said Max. "We figured it would help cheer you up."

"For me?" Abby wasted no time tearing the wrapping away from the package Max handed her. When she caught sight of the painting, she caught her breath. "Oh, my!"

"Well, look at that!" said Grandfather, admiringly. "It's the Ogopogo Resort."

"And look!" Abby cried out with delight. "There's Patch O'Brien's signature in the corner!"

"We found it in the cabin," Adam told her. "So we got it framed."

"Thank you so much!" Abby gave them each a warm hug. "Now I'll have two wonderful treasures."

"Two?" Benny looked puzzled.

"I'm talking about the painting and my wonderful Ogopogo." Abby looked at the carving of Ogopogo beside the fireplace resting on a special wooden stand.

"Omigosh!" exclaimed Jessie.

The others turned to look at her. "What's the matter, Jessie?"

"I know where the treasure is!" she told them in an awestruck voice.

"Where?" Henry wanted to know.

Everyone followed her gaze to the carving of Ogopogo on the wooden stand.

"I don't get it," said Violet. "You think the carving is the treasure? Is that what you mean, Jessie?"

"No, Violet." Jessie shook her head. "I think the treasure's hidden *inside* the carving."

"There's just one catch, Jessie," said Abby. "There's no way Patch could hide anything inside that Ogopogo carving. It's made from solid wood."

"Oh." Jessie's face fell. Still, she couldn't shake the feeling they were on the right track.

Henry had been thinking. "Unless..."

"Unless what, Henry?" Violet wanted to know.

It took Henry a moment to answer.

"Unless the treasure's hidden inside the stand."

"Do you mind if we check it out, Abby?" Jessie asked.

"My grandchildren are seldom wrong when it comes to solving mysteries," Grandfather was quick to add.

"Go for it!" Abby exclaimed as everyone gathered round. "Hurry, I can't stand the suspense!"

"Careful now," said Max, giving Henry a hand. Together, they managed to tip the carving onto its side.

Henry knelt down, then rapped his knuckles against the stand. "Sounds hollow."

Jessie noticed something. "Isn't that a hole on the bottom?" She crouched down beside her older brother to get a closer look.

Henry nodded. "Just big enough for my finger."

"I've got a pencil box with a lid that slides open," said Violet. "Maybe the bottom of the stand slides open, too."

"It's worth a try." Henry stuck his finger

into the hole and pushed with all his might. The base of the stand jerked a little to the side. He pushed again. This time, the base slid far enough to leave a small opening.

"That should do the trick," said Grandfather.

Henry reached into the hollow stand and patted all around.

"Can you feel anything, Henry?" Benny was bouncing from one foot to the other.

Henry shook his head. "I don't—wait!"

Everyone gasped when Henry pulled out a red velvet pouch. "I think this belongs to you, Abby." He stood up straight and held it out to her.

"Oh, my!" cried Abby.

"That's not a very *big* pouch," said Benny, who sounded a bit disappointed.

Jessie smiled over at her little brother. "You know what they say, Benny," she reminded him. "Good things come in small packages."

"Well, let's find out if that old saying is true," said Abby. She took a deep breath,

then shook the contents of the pouch onto the coffee table.

For a moment, no one said a word. They just stared in amazement. Then Violet whispered, "Diamonds!"

Abby sank back against the cushions. "Bless his heart!" she said, in a daze. "Patch really did find treasure on a sunken ship, after all!"

"Those diamonds must be worth a small fortune," said Max.

"You'll have more than enough money to fix up the resort, Abby," Adam told her.

"And pay for some advertising," added Grandfather.

Abby clasped her hands together. "Yes, it looks like I'll be keeping the old place after all."

"Your grandchildren really saved the day, James," said Abby. Her smile made the four Aldens feel warm all over.

But something was still bothering Violet. "If Rilla wasn't behind the Ogopogo hoax, then who was?"

"That was me," Adam said in a small voice.

All eyes turned to him. "What's this all about?" asked Max.

Adam blurted out the truth. "I wanted the Aldens to think they'd seen Ogopogo."

"But...how?" Violet's eyebrows furrowed.

Adam looked over at her. "You're wondering how I did it?"

Violet nodded. "It looked just like—oh!" she cried in sudden understanding. "You used one of Patch's carvings, didn't you?"

Adam didn't deny it. "I put the carving on the raft, and floated it out into the water." Then he glanced over at Abby sheepishly. "I just borrowed it from one of the cabins, Abby. I planned to put it back."

"I don't understand," said Abby. "Why would you try to fool the Aldens?"

"That's what *I'd* like to know," Max added with a frown.

Henry thought he knew the answer to that. "You thought we'd report it to the newspaper, didn't you?"

"I was hoping a sighting would bring tourists into town," Adam confessed.

Jessie nodded in understanding. No wonder Adam seemed to have changed his mind overnight. He didn't believe Ogopogo was real, but he wanted the Aldens to believe it did.

"Oh, I get it," said Max. "You figured if business picked up, then Abby wouldn't sell the resort."

Adam nodded. "I hadn't counted on the Aldens figuring out it was a hoax."

"I know your heart was in the right place, Adam," said Abby. "But it's never a good thing to fool people."

Adam looked truly sorry. "I guess I made a big mistake."

"Everybody makes mistakes." Henry told him. "We'll be here until the end of the week," he added with a friendly smile. "Maybe we can make a fresh start."

Adam smiled. "I'd like that."

Abby looked at Adam. "You made a mistake because you were trying to be a friend, and I'm so lucky to have so many friends care about me so much."

"There's no treasure better than a good friend!" said Benny. "Right?"

"Right!" everyone answered together.

THE VAMPIRE MYSTERY

created by

GERTRUDE CHANDLER WARNER

Illustrated by Robert Papp

ALBERT WHITMAN & Company
Chicago, Illinois

Library of Congress Cataloging-in-Publication Data

Warner, Gertrude Chandler.
The vampire mystery / created by Gertrude Chandler Warner ; illustrated by
Robert Papp.
p. cm. — (The Boxcar children mysteries ; 120)
Summary: When the Aldens agree to watch the house of a local author who
has written a book about a vampire, they end up investigating activities that
are suspiciously similar to those in his book.
ISBN 978-0-8075-8460-6 (hardcover)
ISBN 978-0-8075-8461-3 (pbk.)
[1. Vampires—Fiction. 2. Brothers and sisters—Fiction. 3. Orphans—Fiction.
4. Mystery and detective stories.] I. Papp, Robert, ill. II. Title.
PZ7.W244Vam 2009
[Fic]—dc22
2009018564

Cover art by Robert Papp.

For information about Albert Whitman & Company,
visit our web site at www.albertwhitman.com.

Contents

CHAPTER   PAGE

1. The Greenfield Vampire   1
2. An Offer to Help   11
3. A Missing Book   22
4. Lost!   30
5. A Vial of Blood?   37
6. Accused   46
7. Three Suspects   61
8. Intruder   69
9. A Mysterious Photo   77
10. Caught!   85

THE VAMPIRE MYSTERY

The Greenfield Vampire

"Just this one book please," six-year-old Benny said. He gave *The Legend of the Vampire* to the librarian. On the cover was a picture of a scary man in a dark cape. He had two sharp teeth and blood red lips.

"Oh, Benny, are you sure that is a good book for you?" asked twelve-year-old Jessie. She was twelve and kept an eye on her younger brother. "I could help you pick out another."

"No, I want this one, Jessie," Benny said.

"Henry found it in the local author's section."

"It was written by Mr. Charles Hudson," explained Henry. At fourteen, he was the oldest.

"Oh!" exclaimed ten-year-old Violet. "Is that the author Grandfather told us about this morning?"

"I think it is," Henry said.

Mrs. Skylar, the librarian, smiled at the four Alden children. "Mr. Hudson is a local author who has written many exciting books. *The Legend of the Vampire* is one of his best selling stories. It's set right here in Greenfield."

Violet shivered. "A vampire in Greenfield?" she asked.

"Vampires aren't real, Violet," Jessie said. She put her arm around her sister's shoulders.

"Are you sure?" asked Benny.

"We're sure," Henry said. "Vampires are not real. They're just part of scary stories that people like to read for fun."

"Not real—like ghosts and monsters under your bed?" asked Benny.

"Yes, exactly like that," Jessie said.

"I like scary stories," Benny said. "They always have mysteries in them!" He opened the book to the first page. "'The cem... cem...'" Benny was just learning how to read.

"Cemetery," Henry helped.

"'The cemetery on...'" Benny scratched his forehead.

Violet looked over his shoulder at the page. "Whittaker Street," she told her little brother.

"'Was...dark...and...'" Benny sounded out the words. He sighed. "It's too hard for me. Can you read it to me, Henry?"

"Sure, Benny," Henry said. "But it's getting late now. We promised to meet Grandfather at eleven o'clock."

Jessie looked at her watch. "You're right, Henry." She handed her library card to Mrs. Skylar and checked out her novel. "Grandfather said that he wanted us to meet an old friend of his."

"Do you have the address where Grandfather wants to meet us?" Violet asked.

Henry patted his pocket. "Yes, I have it," he said. "I don't think it's very far. It's on the east end of town."

"Will we be passing any places to eat on the way?" Benny asked hopefully.

"Oh, Benny!" Jessie laughed. Benny had a big appetite. "How can you possibly be hungry after all those pancakes Mrs. McGregor made for you this morning?"

Mrs. McGregor was the Alden's housekeeper. She was a wonderful cook as well.

Benny patted his growling stomach. "I don't know, Jessie," he said. "I guess that's one mystery I'll never be able to solve!"

The Alden children laughed and hopped on their bikes. In ten minutes they found 52 Whittaker Street. It was an old, quaint house with a small lawn and a blooming flower garden. Grandfather's car was parked out front. He stood on the pale lavender porch talking to a tall man with white hair and a white mustache.

"What a beautiful house!" Violet exclaimed. She was wearing a pale purple top that matched the color of the porch almost exactly. It was her favorite color.

"Why, thank you," the man said, smiling at Violet.

Grandfather rested his hand on Benny's shoulder. "Mr. Hudson, I would like to introduce you to my family. This is Henry, Jessie, Violet, and Benny."

After their parents died, the Alden children ran away. They lived in an abandoned boxcar in the woods until their grandfather found them. He brought them to live with him in his big, white house in Greenfield.

"We're very pleased to meet you," Jessie said.

"Mr. Hudson?" Violet's face flushed red. "The famous author?"

Mr. Hudson laughed. "I'm not all that famous, you know," he said.

"You *are* famous!" Benny cried. He pulled *The Legend of the Vampire* from his backpack. "Your book was in the library!"

Just then a big, blue car screeched to a halt in front of the house. A young man in a business suit jumped out. He hurried up the sidewalk.

"This is the last time!" he said. He hammered a "For Sale" sign into the lawn. His face was red.

Grandfather looked puzzled.

"Don't mind Josh," Mr. Hudson said. "He is my realtor and someone keeps stealing his sign from my front lawn. He's been quite upset by it."

Benny looked at Josh banging away on the metal sign. "What's a realtor?" he asked.

"A realtor is a person who tries to help you sell your home," Jessie explained.

"Let me give Josh a hand." Grandfather went over and held the sign steady while Josh hammered.

"Are you moving away from Greenfield, Mr. Hudson?" Henry asked.

"No. I love Greenfield," Mr. Hudson said. "I don't really even want to sell my home." He sighed and looked up at the pretty house. "I've lived here all my life, but it is too big of a place for one old man to take care of on his own. When the house is sold, I'll move to an apartment on the other side of town."

"You mean *if* the house is ever sold," Josh said, wiping his forehead.

"Now, Josh," Mr. Hudson scolded. "Just because the sign keeps disappearing doesn't mean we can't sell the house."

"No, but the broken flowerpots and the old cemetery out back don't help either."

"Old cemetery?" asked Violet.

"Yes," Mr. Hudson replied. "It's quite historic. Some of Greenfield's first citizens are buried back there. You kids are welcome to go take a look. It's actually very beautiful and peaceful."

"Except when the vampire is prowling," Josh added.

The Aldens were too surprised to speak. Violet's face turned white.

"Don't pay attention to Josh," Mr. Hudson hurriedly said. "He gets overly excited sometimes. The vampire is just an old legend."

"But, you said you saw…" Josh tried to argue.

"Now is not the time or place to discuss this, Josh," Mr. Hudson said, glancing over at the Aldens.

"Let's take a walk out back," Jessie said to her sister and brothers. Benny held tightly to Jessie's hand, and Violet stayed close to Henry's side as the Aldens walked back to see the old cemetery. The grass was neatly cut between the rows of the weather-worn headstones.

"What's a legend, anyway?" asked Benny as the children walked.

"It's an old story that has become famous," Jessie said.

"Like Paul Bunyan and his big blue ox," Henry said. "That story is a legend."

Just then the Aldens heard a loud sound in the quiet cemetery. They stopped walking and stared at each other.

Benny groaned. "I'm sorry. I can't help it," he said. "I'm so hungry my stomach keeps growling."

Henry laughed. "I think your appetite is becoming a legend, Benny."

"I know," Benny said. "Right now I think I could eat more than both Paul Bunyan and his ox!"

Violet bent over to look at an old headstone with a pretty flower carved on its front. "This one is hundreds of years old," she said. "The person buried here died in 1742." As she stood up, something caught her eye at the edge of the cemetery.

"Look!" Violet gripped Henry's arm. "There's someone staring at us over there!"

Henry, Jessie, and Benny turned just in time to see the man. He wore a long, dark coat. When he saw that the children had spotted him, he ducked behind a tree and disappeared into the woods.

Violet shivered. "That was odd," she said.

"Not really, Violet," said Henry. "Maybe he was just taking a walk, the same as we were."

"I'm sure Henry's right," Jessie said. "But let's get back to Grandfather now."

CHAPTER 2

An Offer to Help

"What do you think of our little cemetery?" Mr. Hudson asked as the children stepped back onto the porch.

"It is quiet and peaceful," Jessie said. "Just like you said it would be."

Josh was rocking back and forth on a squeaky wooden rocking chair in the corner. He glanced at Jessie then quickly looked away and bit down on his lower lip.

"I sure hope you will all stay for some lunch," said Mr. Hudson.

"Lunch? You bet!" cried Benny. "What are we having?"

"Oh, Benny, that's not polite," Jessie said.

"I'm sorry, Mr. Hudson. I didn't mean to be rude." Benny sniffed the air. "But I can smell something really good."

Mr. Hudson laughed. "It tastes as good as it smells, Benny. That's my famous red clam chowder cooking on the stove. I made a big pot of it and I have a plate of sandwiches as well."

"Clam chowder!" Benny said. "That's my favorite!"

Jessie and Benny set the table, and Henry and Violet poured tall glasses of lemonade for everyone. The kitchen had wide oak floors and pretty flowered curtains on the windows.

"Your home is so beautiful, Mr. Hudson," Violet said.

"Thank you, Violet." Mr. Hudson filled her bowl with hot soup. "I do hate to sell it. It is filled with so many memories. My parents moved here years ago before I was even born. They hoped that the house would always stay in our family."

"Did you write all your books here, Mr. Hudson?" asked Henry. He took a turkey sandwich and passed the tray to Grandfather.

"Yes, Henry, I did. There's a small room upstairs that looks out over the cemetery and the woods. I started writing stories up there when I was a little boy. I get some of my best ideas when I am looking out that window."

Josh dropped his spoon. "Is that where you were when you saw the vampire?" he said.

Mr. Hudson shook his head. "Now, Josh, I thought we agreed not to talk about such things."

"You agreed. I did not." Josh pushed his chair back from the table. "Until we solve this vampire problem, I don't see how I will be able to sell this house. Mrs. Fairfax says she found blood on her back porch yesterday! Some of the other neighbors have heard strange sounds coming from the cemetery at night. Word is getting around town that the vampire in your book has come to life."

The Alden children looked at each other

across the table. Benny sat very still, the soup spoon frozen at his lips.

"Josh, please stop that vampire talk. You know it is just a story," Mr. Hudson said.

Josh shrugged. "I'm only trying to do my job."

Mr. Hudson shook his head. "I don't think this kind of talk is helping."

Josh stood abruptly. "I'm sorry, but I have to get back to the office, now. Thanks for the lunch, Charles. Call me before you leave," he added. The screen door slammed behind him.

Mr. Hudson sighed. "Josh is so excitable," he said. "I should have hired a nice, calm realtor to sell my house."

"Is there really a vampire around here?" Benny asked.

"Of course not," Grandfather answered. "Vampires are not real."

"Your grandfather is right," Mr. Hudson said. "When I was growing up in this house, there was an old legend about a vampire around here. People said prowled the town at night and brought his victims to the cemetery. During the daytime, he hid in his coffin and slept. I always loved scary stories. As a matter of fact, I used to frighten my little brother by telling him all about the vampire. Sometimes, he was so afraid that he would have to sleep in my bed with me. I thought that the vampire story was so much fun that when I grew up I turned it into a book."

"*The Legend of the Vampire!*" Benny cried. "We checked it out of the library this morning. It's outside in my backpack."

"Yes, Benny. That's the one. It became a popular book. It has been so popular that I am hoping to convince a producer to turn my book into a movie."

"How exciting," said Jessie. "Would it be filmed here in Greenfield?"

Mr. Hudson refilled Benny's bowl with chowder. "I had hoped so," Mr. Hudson said. "I was supposed to go out of town to meet with some people to discuss the project. But with the house for sale, I'm not sure that I can leave just now. There's no one to look after the place while I'm away."

"We would be happy to do it," Henry offered.

"Yes," Jessie added. "We could check on it every day if you like."

"Are you sure?" Mr. Hudson asked. "You really wouldn't mind? I would be happy to pay you."

"We're sure," Violet said. "And you don't have to pay us anything. We can ride our bikes over. I'll water the flowers out front in the garden."

"And I can cut the lawn," Henry said.

"Benny and I will sweep the porch and dust the furniture for you," Jessie said.

Grandfather smiled. "My grandchildren are very helpful."

"I can see that," Mr. Hudson said. "And I'm very grateful. Now I can go away without worrying that I might lose a sale because the house is not in good shape."

After Grandfather left to attend a business meeting, Mr. Hudson walked with the Aldens to the back of the house. He opened the door to the shed. "The lawn mower is a little old," he said to Henry. "Sometimes it acts up."

"Don't worry, Mr. Hudson," Jessie said. "Henry is very good with motors and with fixing things."

The shed was large, but dark. Mr. Hudson called the children over to the corner. He lifted a clay flowerpot from a wooden shelf. "This is where I keep a spare key to the house," he said. "It will be right here under this pot whenever you need to get inside."

"Wow, this is a cool bike," Violet said, running her hand over the shiny front fender of an old-fashioned blue bicycle.

Violet admiring old bicycle.

"Yes," said Mr. Hudson. "It is very old, but I like to keep it in good shape. It belongs to my brother. It's odd, though. I thought that I had stored the bicycle in the back of the shed. I wonder how it got up here?"

"Does your brother live nearby?" asked Benny.

Mr. Hudson dropped his hands into his pockets. He looked at the ground for a few moments before answering. "No. I'm sorry

to say that my brother and I had a fight a long time ago when we were younger. My brother left town and I never heard from him again. It was a silly fight. I don't even remember what it was about anymore. It happened over forty years ago."

Suddenly, everyone heard loud shouts coming from the front of the house. They ran from the shed. An older woman was pointing at the Aldens' bicycles and calling out for Mr. Hudson.

"Look at this!" she cried. "Bicycles are blocking the sidewalk! How am I supposed to get my shopping cart past? I think I hurt my ankle on this one." Mrs. Fairfax pointed at Benny's small bike.

"Hold on, Martha," Mr. Hudson said. "We'll get them out of your way."

Henry, Jessie, Violet, and Benny quickly moved their bicycles onto the lawn. Mrs. Fairfax glared at them.

"We're so sorry," Jessie said. "It was careless of us to leave our bikes there. We hope your ankle doesn't hurt too badly."

"Children are always careless!" Mrs. Fairfax said. "These children aren't moving in here, are they, Charles?" she asked.

"These are the Aldens," Mr. Hudson said. "They are the grandchildren of James Alden, an old friend of mine. They will be looking after my house while I am away on business."

Mrs. Fairfax pushed her glasses up on her nose and stared at each of the Aldens. "Well, you better make sure they don't leave their things lying around in my way."

"We won't do that, Mrs. Fairfax," Henry promised.

Mrs. Fairfax marched up the sidewalk and into her home.

Mr. Hudson sighed. "I'm sorry about that, children," he said. "Mrs. Fairfax is not a bad lady. She was a good friend of my brother's and has lived next door to me for fifty years. But she is worried that I might sell my home to a noisy family with lots of children and barking dogs. She likes her peace and quiet."

"We'll park our bikes behind the house from now on," Henry said. "We should never have left them on the sidewalk."

The four Aldens said goodbye to Mr. Hudson. As they pedaled toward home, they saw Mrs. Fairfax staring at them from the front window of her house.

CHAPTER 3

A Missing Book

After dinner, the Aldens each took a slice of Mrs. McGregor's apple pie and headed outside to the front porch. Watch, their wire-haired terrier, raced outdoors with them.

"How did the smallest Alden end up with the biggest piece of pie?" asked Henry.

Benny, his cheeks stuffed with the delicious dessert, shrugged his shoulders.

"Henry," asked Violet, "what do you really think about the vampire story? It seems like Mr. Hudson did see something in the cemetery that scared him."

"I'm sure the vampire's not real, Violet. But something odd does seem to be going on at Mr. Hudson's house."

"Yes," said Jessie. "Why would someone steal the 'For Sale' sign on his front lawn?"

"I'm not sure," said Henry. "Maybe it was just a joke."

Violet shook her head. "Josh certainly wasn't laughing."

"No," Jessie replied. "And Josh seemed really upset by the vampire story. I wish we knew a little more about that legend. It might help us to solve the mystery of what is going on at Mr. Hudson's house."

Benny jumped from his chair and dashed into the house. He returned with his backpack. Watch barked excitedly.

"Benny, what are you doing?" asked Jessie.

"It's a clue!" Benny replied. "The book I got at the library yesterday that Mr. Hudson wrote. I put it in my backpack."

"That's right, Benny!" Henry said. "I had forgotten about *The Legend of the Vampire*."

"And didn't Mr. Hudson say that he based his book on the old vampire legend?" asked Violet.

"Yes, he did," said Jessie. "Good work, Benny."

Benny reached into his backpack. A funny look came over his face.

"What's wrong?" asked Jessie.

"I know I put the book in my backpack," he said. "But now it's not here."

"Maybe you took it out when you got home," suggested Violet.

"No, I'm sure I didn't," Benny said.

"Could it have fallen out?" asked Jessie.

"I don't think so," Benny said. "There are no holes in my backpack. But maybe I didn't zip it closed all the way."

"We should ride our bikes back to the library and to Mr. Hudson's," Henry suggested. "We can look along the streets to check if the book fell out."

Henry, Jessie, Violet, and Benny strapped on their helmets and rode to the library. It was almost closing time.

"Hello, children," said Mrs. Skylar. "The library will be closing in about ten minutes. Can I help you find something?"

"No, thank you, Mrs. Skylar," said Henry. "We were wondering if anyone turned in *The Legend of the Vampire*."

Mrs. Skylar went to her computer and clicked the keys. "No," she said. "The computer shows that it was checked out this morning by Benny. Did something happen to the book?"

"We seem to have misplaced it," said Jessie. "But I'm sure we'll find it soon."

"I hope so," said Mrs. Skylar. "Good luck."

"Don't look so sad, Benny," said Jessie. "We still might find the book outside Mr. Hudson's house."

The four Aldens rode quickly through Greenfield until they arrived at Whittaker Street. It was still light out, but the sun was beginning to set behind Mr. Hudson's house.

The woods and the cemetery were full of shadows.

Henry, Jessie, Violet, and Benny spread out and searched the sidewalk and the lawn. There was no sign of the book.

"Maybe Mr. Hudson found it already," Violet suggested. "He might have the book inside."

Henry knocked on the door, but no one answered. It was very quiet.

Suddenly, a loud clatter came from the side yard. The children ran to the edge of the porch. Their bicycles were lying in a heap on the ground.

"That's odd," said Henry.

"Maybe it was the wind," Violet suggested.

Benny jumped over the porch rail and picked up his bike. "It's not very windy." Something caught his eye and he pointed toward the cemetery. "Look!"

"What do you see?" asked Jessie.

But whatever it was, it was gone.

"I don't know," Benny said. "I thought I saw someone in a dark cape running. But I

guess it was just a shadow."

"We should get home," Henry said. "Grandfather doesn't like us riding our bikes in the dark. And it is getting late."

"But what about the book?" asked Benny. "We still haven't found it."

"Don't worry," said Jessie. "If we don't find it by the due date, we'll all chip in from our allowance money to pay for the book."

"Hey! Is that you Alden children over there making all that clatter?" Mrs. Fairfax was leaning against the rail of her front porch.

"We're sorry," Henry called. "The wind knocked our bicycles over. We're leaving now."

"I hope so," she said, turning away and stomping back toward her front door. "A person can't get any peace around here. And stop running through my backyard!"

"But we…" Violet wanted to explain that they had not run through her yard, but Mrs. Fairfax was already inside, the screen door slamming shut behind her.

"Why is she so angry?" asked Benny.

"Mrs. Fairfax probably just likes her peace and quiet," Violet said. "I suppose she's not used to such noises on this street. Maybe we frightened her."

"I hope I don't upset her when I have to cut the lawn," Henry added. "Lawn mowers make plenty of noise."

"So does my stomach," said Benny. "All this bike riding has made me hungry."

Henry laughed. "Let's go home and get you another piece of Mrs. McGregor's pie."

CHAPTER 4

Lost!

The next morning Mrs. McGregor placed a large platter of steaming waffles on the breakfast table.

"Here you go, Benny," she said. "I made a special waffle for you."

Benny had been sitting with his head in his hands. He looked up to see what Mrs. McGregor had made. It was a large round waffle with strawberries for eyes and a blueberry mouth. Fluffy white whipped cream hair sat on top.

"Wow! Thank you, Mrs. McGregor." Benny grabbed his fork.

"There's the smile we like to see," said Grandfather. "Are you feeling better now?"

Benny's mouth was stuffed full with waffle and fruit.

Jessie answered for him. "Benny's not sick, Grandfather. He feels badly because he can't find *The Legend of the Vampire*, the book he checked out of the library yesterday."

"Perhaps it's in your room, Benny," Grandfather suggested.

Benny shook his head.

Violet spooned fruit over her waffle. "We searched everywhere," she said.

"It was in his backpack when we were at Mr. Hudson's house. By the time we got home, it had mysteriously disappeared. We even checked at the library to see if anyone had turned it in." Henry poured himself a glass of orange juice.

"That *is* a mystery," Grandfather said. "But I'm sure you children will figure it out."

The Aldens loved mysteries and they had already solved quite a few since coming to live with Grandfather.

"Maybe you can check at the library again today," Grandfather said. "They are having their annual fair and bake sale on the front lawn. It might be fun to stop by."

A timer in the kitchen rang. "That must be my pie," Mrs. McGregor said, wiping her hands on her apron. "I made an apple pie and a lemon cake to donate to the bake sale. If you children want, you can come with me this morning when I drop them off at the library."

"That reminds me," Grandfather said. "Mr. Hudson called this morning. He will be leaving on his business trip shortly. He asked if you children could stop by the house later today to cut the lawn and make sure everything is neat and in order. A young couple from out of town will be stopping by to look at the house this afternoon. Mr. Hudson is hoping that they will be interested in buying it."

"Are you sure Mr. Hudson called this morning?" asked Henry. "We thought he might have left for his trip last night."

"No," Grandfather said. "It was this morning. He said he was packing his bags as he spoke to me."

"We'll go to Mr. Hudson's after the library," Henry said.

"It's such a beautiful house," Violet added. "We'll make sure it is in good shape when that couple arrives. I'm sure they'll love it."

Henry, Jessie, Violet, and Benny helped Mrs. McGregor with the dishes and then carefully placed the baked goods in the car.

"The car smells so good!" Benny exclaimed as Mrs. McGregor drove into town.

Violet laughed. "You're right, Benny. It smells like a bakery in here."

Mrs. McGregor parked the car by the curb across the street from the library. Henry carried the apple pie and Jessie took the lemon cake.

Balloons were everywhere. They were tied to the tables and the street lamps and to the backs of chairs. Colorful streamers hung from the library windows and rippled in the wind. On one side of the lawn, a man with a beard played a guitar while children sang along. A storyteller in a long dress sat in a circle and used puppets to tell her tale.

"Hello!" Mrs. Skylar called. "I'm so glad you could come to the library fair."

"We wouldn't think of missing it," Mrs. McGregor said.

"Mrs. McGregor made this cake and the pie," Jessie explained. "They're for the bake sale table."

"They look beautiful!" Mrs. Skylar exclaimed. "I'm sure we'll get a very large donation for them."

Mrs. McGregor beamed.

"Do you think this is a big enough donation for Mrs. McGregor's lemon cake?" Benny pulled a fist from his pocket. He opened his hand to show three nickels, a dime, two quarters, a rubber band, a gum wrapper, and a small rock.

Mrs. McGregor laughed. "Oh, Benny,"

she said. "I can make another lemon cake for you at home."

Henry plucked the rock and the gum wrapper from Benny's hand. He chuckled. "I don't think these are worth very much, Benny," he said.

"The rock does have pretty colors in it, though." Violet smiled at her little brother.

"Why don't we take the pie and the cake over to the bake-sale table for Mrs. McGregor," Jessie suggested. "Maybe you can buy some cookies or a cupcake with your coins."

"Okay. Let's go!" Benny darted off through the crowd.

"Benny! Wait for us!" Henry called. But it was too late. Thinking only of cookies, Benny had run far ahead.

Henry, Jessie, and Violet said goodbye to Mrs. McGregor and thanked her for the ride to the library fair. Then they headed toward the bake sale. They set Mrs. McGregor's pie and cake on the table.

"Where's Benny?" asked Jessie.

"I don't know," Henry replied. "I thought for sure we would see him here picking out some cookies."

"Excuse me," Violet said to the lady behind the table. "Was there a six-year-old boy with dark-brown hair here a few moments ago?"

"The table has been crowded," the lady said. "I'm not sure. Is that him over there?" She pointed through the crowd.

Violet ran toward the little boy, but it was not Benny.

Henry and Jessie looked worried.

"Maybe he couldn't find the bake-sale table," Violet said. "He's probably wandering nearby."

"Let's split up," Henry said. "We'll each go a different way and meet back here in ten minutes."

"Benny! Benny!" Henry, Jessie, and Violet ran through the crowd calling their brother's name. But he was nowhere in sight.

CHAPTER 5

A Vial of Blood?

Jessie found Benny walking down the sidewalk. There was a scrape on his knee and a trickle of blood running down his leg.

"Benny!" she cried, "Where have you been? We were so worried. What happened to your leg?"

Just then, Henry and Violet came running up to them.

Jessie settled Benny on a soft patch of grass under a tree. Violet ran to borrow the first-aid kit from Mrs. Skylar.

"Are you okay?" Henry asked.

Benny nodded bravely. He was almost as breathless as Violet when she returned with the first-aid kit.

Jessie cleaned the blood from his knee and squirted a bit of antiseptic on his cut. She covered it up with a bandage.

"I was running to the bake-sale table," Benny said. "I guess I wasn't watching where I was going. I crashed smack into a man and I fell to the ground."

"Is that how you hurt your knee?" Violet asked.

Benny nodded. "The man leaned down to help me up. I was so surprised. It was Mr. Hudson!"

"Mr. Hudson?" Henry said. "But he's away on his business trip. Are you sure it was him?"

Benny scratched his head. "Now I'm not so sure. I thought so at first. I called him Mr. Hudson when I apologized. When I said that name, he looked upset. He turned and left really fast."

"But where have you been?" asked Jessie.

"We looked all over for you."

"I followed him," Benny said.

"Benny! You shouldn't have done that. You should have stayed here by the library," Jessie said.

"I know. I'm sorry, Jessie. But the man dropped something. I tried to catch up with him so I could give it back. I didn't go far."

"Did you catch him?" asked Violet.

"No. He had an old blue bike down the street behind a tree. He rode away."

"What did he drop?" asked Henry.

Benny held out his hand. "This," he said.

Henry took the small plastic bottle from his brother. It was filled with a red liquid.

"What do you think it could be?" Jessie asked.

"I don't know," said Henry.

"I do," said Violet, putting her hand to her mouth. "It looks like…like…blood!"

The Alden children stared at each other for a few seconds. "I know it looks like blood," Henry said. "But it is probably something else. It could be ink."

"Or medicine," Jessie added. "Remember your cough syrup from last winter, Violet? It was red."

"I suppose that's true," Violet said. "But that is an odd bottle for cough medicine."

Henry put the bottle in his pocket. "I'll hold onto it in case we see the man again."

"Let's go to the diner," Jessie said. "I think we could all use a cool drink and some time to think."

"And some food!" Benny added.

It was lunch time, and the diner was very crowded. Nancy, a thin waitress with short blond hair, showed the Aldens to a booth in the back.

"How's this kids?" she asked.

"It's perfect. Thank you," said Jessie.

After they had placed their order, Jessie pulled out her notebook and a pencil. When facing a mystery, the Aldens often found that writing all the facts and clues on paper helped them to see what was going on.

Jessie wrote "Vampire Legend" at the top of the page. "What do we know about the

vampire legend?" she asked.

Henry took a long drink of his lemonade. "People around Greenfield used to tell stories about a vampire. We know that vampires are not real, so the people must have done it for fun or to scare each other."

"And Mr. Hudson heard those stories when he was growing up. He turned them into a book," Violet added.

"Then Mr. Hudson saw a vampire in the cemetery behind his house." Benny leaned across the table, his eyes wide.

"No, Benny. He saw something that concerned him. He didn't actually see a vampire," Henry said.

"Then what did he see?" asked Benny.

"We're not sure," Henry said.

Nancy stopped at the table with an armful of plates. "Here you go, kids," she said, setting down the plates of burgers and sandwiches.

Violet chewed thoughtfully on her grilled cheese. "One thing we do know," she said. "Mr. Hudson is trying to sell his house, but strange things are happening there that keep buyers away."

Jessie made a list. "There was the 'vampire' in the cemetery," she said. "And the broken flowerpots on the front porch."

"And someone keeps stealing the 'For Sale' sign." Violet finished her sandwich and placed her napkin on her plate.

"But why would anyone care if Mr. Hudson sold his house?" asked Benny.

"Mrs. Fairfax does not want him to move," Jessie said.

"That's true," Henry replied. "Do you think she could be the one behind all the strange happenings?"

Benny suddenly sat up very straight. "It's him," he whispered. "The man from the library."

"Where?" asked Henry who was across the table from Benny and facing the opposite direction.

"He's at the other end of the diner, sitting at the counter. I could give him back his bottle of blood...I mean, red stuff." Benny slid out of the booth. "Hurry, Henry. Give it to me. He's just about to leave."

Henry reached into his pocket, but it was too late. The man quickly jumped off his stool, his head lowered into his shirt, and darted out of the diner.

A few minutes later, Nancy stopped at the table to clear the plates. "Would you like to order dessert?" she asked.

"No, thank you," Jessie answered. "Not today."

"Excuse me," Henry asked. "Did you happen to wait on the man who was at the end of the counter? The one who left a few minutes ago?"

Nancy looked toward the empty stool. "Yes, I did," she answered. "Why do you want to know?"

"We have something of his," Henry said. "He dropped it earlier today and we wanted to give it back. Do you know where we can find him?"

"No," Nancy replied. "I'm sorry. I never saw him before. But it's odd that you say that. I have something for him too. He left the diner so quickly that he forgot to take his book with him."

"His book?" asked Violet.

"Yes." Nancy reached into the deep pocket of her apron. "It's a library book. He left it on the counter beside his plate."

She set the book on the table.

Jessie gasped. "*The Legend of the Vampire!*"

Benny pulled the book toward him and stared down at the blood red fangs of the man on the cover. "We could take it back to the library for you," he offered.

"Why, thanks," said Nancy. "I appreciate that. It will save me a trip. If the man comes back, I'll tell him that his book is at the library. Have a good day, kids."

When Nancy had left, Benny leaned across the table. "It's not *his* book. It's mine!"

CHAPTER 6

Accused

The Aldens walked slowly to Mr. Hudson's house on Whittaker Street.

"I don't understand why he would take Benny's book," Jessie said.

"Maybe it was an accident," Violet offered. "Maybe the book dropped out of Benny's bag and the man found it."

The children had no more time to talk. As they turned the corner onto Whittaker Street, they saw police cars in front of Mr. Hudson's house!

"There they are! They're the ones who did it!" Mrs. Fairfax stood on the sidewalk pointing at the Aldens.

The police turned to look at the children. A tall officer with black hair held a pad and a pen. "Excuse me, but who are you?" he asked

"We're the Aldens," Henry said. He introduced himself and his sisters and brother. "Is something wrong, Officer?"

Officer Franklin wrote their names on his pad. Then he looked up. "Someone vandalized this house last night."

"Oh, my!" Violet cried. A number of Mr. Hudson's beautiful flowers had been ripped from the ground and were lying across the walkway.

Benny was the first to see the words written across the porch boards in bright red letters. "'Leave...me...to...rest...in...pea...pea...'" He turned to Henry for help.

"'Leave me to rest in peace,'" Henry read. "'Or you will be sorry.'"

"It was those children who did it!" Mrs. Fairfax said. "I saw them here last night.

They were right there on the porch."

Officer Franklin looked at Henry. "Were you here last night?" he asked.

"Yes, officer," Henry replied. "But we sure didn't do this."

"Then what were you doing here?" the officer asked.

Just then the front door of Mr. Hudson's house opened. Josh rushed out.

"Thank goodness you children are here!" he said.

"You know them?" Officer Franklin asked Josh.

"Of course!" Josh replied. "These are the Aldens. Mr. Hudson told me that they would be stopping by today."

"And you don't suspect that they could have caused this damage?" the officer asked.

"What? No! Of course not. Mr. Hudson trusts them and so do I. He asked them to look after his place while he was away."

"Sorry, children," Officer Franklin said. "I hope you understand that it is my job to ask questions."

LEAVE ME TO REST
in Peace Or
you will Be Sorry

"We understand," Henry said.

Mrs. Fairfax banged her cane against the ground. "Seems to me you don't ask enough questions!" she said. "This used to be a nice, quiet street until that realtor and those children started coming around. They're up to something. You need to investigate them!" She stomped back to her house.

Josh ran his hands through his hair. "What am I going to do?" he asked. "The Bensons will be here in a few hours to look at the house. When they see this, they will never want to buy it."

"We'll clean it up," Jessie said. "We'll start right away."

"No," Josh said. "We can't clean it up. It is evidence. The police might need it. We should leave everything just the way it is."

Officer Franklin overheard them. "It's okay for you children to clean up the mess," he said. "We have taken pictures of every-thing. That is all we need."

Josh bit down on his lower lip and kicked at one of the upturned plants. "Are you sure?"

he asked. "We want you to find the person who did this."

"I'm sure," Officer Franklin replied. "We have all the information that we need."

The police officers left and Josh dropped onto the porch steps. "This is too much," he said.

"What do you mean?" asked Henry.

"Don't you see?" Josh asked. "It's the vampire!"

"But there's no such thing," Jessie said.

Josh's face was white. "It's right from the book," he said. "I've read it."

"*The Legend of the Vampire?*" asked Benny.

"Yes," Josh answered. "In the book, a vampire has his coffin hidden in the basement of an old home. A lonely old man lives by himself in the house. There is a cemetery behind the house. The vampire only comes out at night when the old man is sleeping. But one day the old man decides to sell the house. The vampire does not want his peace disturbed. He bites the neck of anyone who comes to live in the house."

Violet shivered. "What a terrible story!"

"What happens in the end?" Benny asked.

"No one will live in the house," Josh said. "The vampire has it all to himself." Josh looked over his shoulder and lowered his voice. "And the vampire still roams the cemetery every night!"

Jessie put her arm around Benny. "But it's just a story!" she said. "Everyone knows that vampires are not real."

Josh looked down. "I guess you're right, Jessie," he said. He grabbed an uprooted plant that was sitting on the step and tossed it angrily onto the lawn.

Violet picked it up.

"We should get to work," Henry said. "I need to cut the lawn."

"I'll replace the flowers the best that I can," Violet promised.

Jessie stared at the red letters on the porch. "I'll take care of cleaning that."

"What about me?" asked Benny.

Henry put his hand on Benny's shoulder. "Come with me, Benny," he said. "You can rake up the grass as I cut it."

"And I've got to make some phone calls." Josh stood and pulled a cell phone from his pocket. He pointed to the front lawn. "Can you believe that someone stole the 'For Sale' sign again? I'm running out of signs. I'm not sure that I even have any left."

The Aldens walked around to the shed to find the tools they needed. After the bright sunshine, the shed seemed very dark.

"Ouch!" Henry cried.

"Are you okay?" asked Jessie.

"Yes… I just stubbed my toe on the bike," Henry said.

"I don't remember the bike being in that spot yesterday," Violet said.

Henry wheeled the bike to the corner. "You're right, Violet. I think it was on the other side of the shed yesterday. That's odd."

Violet felt something fall down her neck. She cried out.

"What is it, Violet?" asked Jessie. "Are you okay?"

Violet laughed. "Yes," she said. "I guess I'm

a little jumpy. It's the chain for the light bulb. I must have backed into it. It tickled the back of my neck." Violet pulled the chain several times. It clicked, but nothing happened.

"The bulb must be out," said Henry.

"It's okay," Violet replied. "I've found the trowel and some gardening gloves. That's all I need. I'm going to go put those plants back in the ground right away. I don't want the roots to dry out and die. I know how proud Mr. Hudson is of his flowers."

There was a crash against the side of the shed. "I've found the rake!" Benny cried. "I'm all ready to help you, Henry."

Violet carried her tools to the front yard. She decided to work on the plants closest to the porch first. She knelt down and began to dig. She could hear Josh talking on his cell phone inside the house. His voice got louder as he came closer to the screen door on the porch.

"Yes," Josh said. "Mr. Hudson will have to lower the price now. Who will want to buy a house that has a vampire in the backyard?"

Then he laughed. "No," he said. "I don't really believe in vampires. But this is working out very well for us. When Mr. Hudson comes back from his trip, I will convince him that he should offer his house for much less money. Then you can buy it."

Violet stood up. What was Josh talking about?

"Violet!" Josh said. He quickly flipped his cell phone closed. "I didn't see you there! He walked out onto the porch.

"I'm sorry," Violet said. "I didn't mean to startle you. I was replanting the flowers."

Josh stuck his hands deep into his pockets. He looked around the corner of the house. "Are the others still out back?" he asked.

"Yes," Violet said.

"You shouldn't sneak around like that," Josh said. "Especially not with all the things that are going on around here."

"I wasn't sneaking," Violet tried to explain, but Josh's cell phone buzzed.

He looked at the number on the screen, but he did not answer it. He rubbed his stomach instead. "I am so hungry," he said. "I think I will walk over to the diner for a sandwich."

Henry pushed the lawn mower to the front yard. Benny pulled the rake behind him.

"This is going to be fun!" Benny said. "I wish there was a yard full of leaves for me to rake. Then I could make a big pile and jump in it."

"You'll have to wait a few weeks for the leaves to fall," Henry said.

"I'm going to ask Mr. Hudson if I can come back then and rake for him," Benny said.

Henry smiled. "I'm sure he would like that. But maybe he will have sold his house by then."

Violet was about to tell Henry about the person Josh had been speaking to on his cell phone. But just then Henry pulled the cord on the lawn mower. It roared to life.

"Sorry for the noise, Violet!" Henry shouted. "I will try to stay away from the flowers!"

Jessie had gone into the house and found a bucket and a scrub brush. A bottle of cleaner was under the kitchen sink. She filled the bucket with hot soapy water. Then she set to work trying to clean the red words from the porch.

Violet carefully placed the flowers back into the garden. Some of their stems were broken. It made her sad. She smoothed the loose dirt around each plant. Then she found a watering can in the shed and gave each plant a drink. She worked so hard that she forgot all about the conversation that she had overheard.

Mrs. Fairfax came out on her front porch every once in a while. She watched the Aldens with a wary look on her face. But the children were careful not to make too much noise and to stay off Mrs. Fairfax's property.

"There," Henry said, brushing loose grass from his jeans. "I think the house looks fine now."

"I don't know, Henry." Jessie shook her head. "The lawn looks nice and the flowers are beautiful. But I could not wash the letters off completely. If you look closely, you can still read what it says."

Henry walked up the steps to the porch. "I see what you mean. The porch might need to be repainted."

"We could never do that in time. The buyers will be here soon." Jessie sighed.

"I know what we can do!" Benny flung the door open and ran into the house. He returned a minute later. "How about this?" he asked. He held up a small rug.

"Great thinking, Benny!" Henry said.

"I remembered that it was in the kitchen by the sink," Benny said. "It will look nice out here, too."

Jessie took the rug and spread it in front of the porch door. "It doesn't cover everything," she said. "But it is a big improvement. Way to go, Benny."

Jessie locked the door and put the key back under the pot in the shed. Henry tied the bag of grass clippings and walked it to the curb.

"Isn't this Josh's car?" Henry asked.

"Yes," Violet answered. "Josh hasn't left yet. He walked to the diner for a sandwich about a half an hour ago."

"What's that in the back seat?" asked Benny.

The windows were up, but the Aldens could see something large in the back of Josh's car. Most of it was covered with a blanket. But two black metal stakes poked out from beneath the covering.

"It looks like a 'For Sale' sign is under that blanket," Jessie said.

The Aldens were puzzled.

"I thought Josh said he didn't have any more signs left," said Henry.

"It could be for a different house," Violet said. "I'm sure Josh has more than one house to sell. Or maybe it is a 'For Rent' sign for an apartment."

"You could be right, Violet," said Jessie.

Just then Josh came hurrying up the street. "What are you kids doing?" he called crossly. Josh quickly stood in front of his car with his hands on his hips.

"We're only putting the trash bag to the curb," Benny said. "Look at the lawn. Don't you think it looks good? I raked it!"

Josh's face relaxed. "Yes, Benny," he said. "Everything looks very nice again. Thank you. The Bensons should be here soon."

Jessie decided not to tell Josh about the red letters that did not wash off the porch. He still seemed too upset. He leaned back against his car and crossed his arms. His foot tapped nervously against the curb. And maybe Josh and the Bensons would not notice the few faint words that were not covered up by the rug.

The Aldens said goodbye to Josh and headed home.

CHAPTER 7

Three Suspects

Grandfather arrived for dinner just as Mrs. McGregor was setting a pot roast on the table.

"Smells great!" Grandfather said. "I'm sorry I'm late. My meeting lasted longer than I had thought."

Just then, there was a loud clap of thunder, and the lights flickered off and on for a minute. Rain drummed against the side of the house. The children quickly closed all the windows.

"You got home just in time, Grandfather." Violet spread her napkin on her lap. "One moment later and you would have been caught in the storm."

"That's true. My timing was perfect." Grandfather smiled. "I'm glad my grandchildren are not out in this storm."

During dinner, the children told Grandfather about the vandalism at Mr. Hudson's home and the work that they had done to clean it up.

"That was very kind of you," Grandfather said. "I wonder who would do such a thing?"

"We've been wondering the same thing, Grandfather," said Henry.

Jessie spooned some warm applesauce onto Benny's plate. "We think that whoever it is does not want Mr. Hudson to sell his house."

Violet was thinking hard. She'd heard Josh on the phone the day before. She knew he had said something about selling the house. But she couldn't remember what he'd said.

Grandfather shook his head. "I suppose

the vandalism is why Mr. Hudson cut short his business trip."

"Mr. Hudson is home?" asked Henry.

"I thought so." Grandfather passed the mashed potatoes to Benny. "But I could be wrong. Driving home this evening, I thought I saw Mr. Hudson walking down the street near the library. I called out to him, but he turned a corner and disappeared."

After dinner, Grandfather went into his study to make some phone calls. Mrs. McGregor brought out an iced lemon cake and four plates.

"You brought home the lemon cake from the bake sale?" Benny clapped his hands.

"No, Benny," Mrs. McGregor replied. "Someone bought that cake and donated twenty dollars to the library for it."

"Twenty dollars! That must have been the biggest donation at the bake sale!" Violet smiled at Mrs. McGregor.

Mrs. McGregor's face flushed red with pride. "I don't know about that," she said.

"I don't think twenty dollars is enough."

Benny held out his empty plate. "I would pay one hundred dollars for your lemon cake!"

"That's why I made another one for you when I came home." Mrs. McGregor laughed. "And I'll even waive the hundred-dollar fee!"

The Aldens each ate a big slice of the good cake.

"Do you think the man that Grandfather saw today was Mr. Hudson?" asked Violet.

"I don't know," Henry said. "If it was Mr. Hudson, why didn't he say hello when Grandfather called out to him?"

"Maybe he didn't hear Grandfather," said Jessie.

"I thought I saw Mr. Hudson, too," said Benny. "But now I know it wasn't him."

"How do you know?" Jessie refilled Benny's glass with milk.

"The man I saw did not dress like Mr. Hudson. His clothes were old and not very clean. There was dirt on them and even some stains that looked like oil."

Violet tapped her fork on the table,

thinking. "You're probably right, Benny. Mr. Hudson seems to be a very neat person. I don't think he would wear dirty clothes."

Benny took a big gulp of milk. "He did look like Mr. Hudson, but it was probably just his white hair and mustache that confused me."

"I wonder if the Bensons showed up to look at the house this afternoon," Jessie said.

Benny wiped away his milk mustache. "I hope that Josh didn't say anything about vampires to them."

"Josh wouldn't do that," Henry said. "Not if he wants to sell the house for Mr. Hudson. Doesn't he want everyone to be interested in buying it?"

This reminded Violet of something. Something important. Suddenly she remembered what Josh had said on the phone. "Maybe he doesn't!" Violet said.

Henry, Jessie, and Benny looked very surprised.

"Why not, Violet?" asked Jessie. "Selling the house is Josh's job."

At last Violet told the others about the

conversation she had overheard. "He told the person on the phone that everything was working out well. When Mr. Hudson came back from his trip, Josh would convince him to lower the price for the house."

"That is very suspicious," Henry admitted.

Jessie crossed her arms. "And Josh did act strange when he noticed us standing next to his car."

"He knows all about the legend of the vampire," Benny added. "Remember how he told us the whole story?"

"Maybe Josh is behind the vandalism," Henry said. "He could be using scenes from the book to scare people away. If no one wants to buy the house, Mr. Hudson will have to offer it for a very low price."

Violet nodded. "And the person who Josh was speaking to on the phone would get a great house for not much money. That would be so unfair!"

"Maybe if we read Mr. Hudson's book, we can find more clues to this mystery," Henry said. "We might be able to find out what Josh will be up to next."

"If it *is* Josh, that is," Jessie added. "But what if it's Mrs. Fairfax? She doesn't want the house sold either. And since she lives next door, it would be easy for her to cause the damage and sneak back home."

"That's true." Violet folded her napkin. "And Mrs. Fairfax always hears us when we are at Mr. Hudson's house. Don't you think she would have heard the person who broke the flowerpots and wrote on the porch?"

"There is another suspect as well," Henry said. "We shouldn't forget about the man who ran into Benny at the library fair."

"But what could he have to do with it?" asked Benny.

Henry looked thoughtful. "I don't really know. But it is suspicious that he ran away from you when you called him by Mr. Hudson's name. And don't forget that he had your library book. He must have taken it from your backpack at Mr. Hudson's while we were inside having lunch."

"The book! It's gone again! I can't believe

it!" Benny slapped the side of his head.

"What's wrong?" asked Jessie.

"I left it on the kitchen table at Mr. Hudson's house. I set it down there so I could pull up the rug to use to cover the words written on the front porch. Afterwards, I forgot to go back inside for the book."

Henry laughed. "I think there is something mysterious about that book. It never stays in the same place."

"Can we go get it?" asked Benny.

"I suppose we can," said Henry. "But it will be dark soon. We can't ride our bikes."

Violet looked out the window. "The rain seems to have stopped."

The children cleaned up their dessert plates and put the cake away. They each found a flashlight to take on their nighttime walk. The air was slightly cool and the storm clouds were moving away. A round, full moon shone over Greenfield.

CHAPTER 8

Intruder

"What's that?" Violet asked as the children walked up Whittaker Street. "Did you see that light in Mr. Hudson's house?

The others had not seen it. "Maybe it was the moon shining on the window glass," Jessie suggested.

Violet was not so sure. But now the light was gone.

The rain had made the ground wet and muddy. The children's shoes squished in the lawn as they made their way toward the shed to retrieve the key to the house.

They each flicked on their flashlights. Jessie shone her beam on the shed door. Henry lifted the latch and the door squeaked open. The four Aldens stepped into the dark shed.

"Careful," Jessie warned. "Don't trip over the bicycle again."

"That's odd." Henry pointed his flashlight at the bike. "Didn't we move the bike to the left side of the shed today?"

"We did," Jessie agreed.

"Well, now it is on the right side of the shed."

Benny stood beside the bike. "And it's wet!" He shone his flashlight on the roof above the bike. "Even though there aren't any leaks in the roof."

"Someone has been riding this bike." Henry ran his hand over the dripping handlebars.

Violet walked over to look at the bike, but stumbled over an old suitcase. "What is this doing in the middle of the floor?"

"A suitcase?" Benny grabbed the handle

and moved the suitcase against the wall. It was heavy. "Wouldn't Mr. Hudson have taken his suitcase with him when he went on his trip?"

"It looks old," Henry said. "Maybe Mr. Hudson has a newer one that he uses."

Jessie shone her light on the flowerpot. She lifted it up. "It's gone!" she cried. "The key is not here. I know I put it right back under this pot before we left this afternoon."

"Are you sure?" Henry felt around on a lower shelf. "Maybe it fell down here."

Violet and Benny searched the floor.

"I'm positive," Jessie said. "Someone has taken it!"

The Aldens hurried from the shed. They quickly shut and latched the door and ran to the front of the house.

"Look at this!" Benny did not even need his flashlight. In the light of the moon, the children could clearly see a set of muddy footprints leading right up to Mr. Hudson's front door!

Henry put his hand carefully on the doorknob and turned. It was not locked. He entered the house. "Hello! Mr. Hudson! Are you home?" Henry turned to the others. "There's no one here."

"Let's get Benny's book and get home," Violet said.

Jessie flipped the light switch, but nothing happened. "The lights are out!"

"It's probably the circuit breaker," Henry said. "Sometimes a storm can shut it off, especially in an old house like this. I know where the switch is. Mr. Hudson pointed it out when he was showing me around the house. I might be able to get the lights back on."

Henry and Jessie carefully walked down the stairs into the basement. Violet and Benny waited by the front door.

"Did you hear that?" Violet asked, looking over her shoulder.

Benny cocked his head. "Yes. It sounds like footsteps. Do you think it could be Henry and Jessie?"

"No," Violet whispered. "I think it is

coming from outside. I wish Henry and Jessie would hurry up."

"You don't think it could be the vampire, do you?" asked Benny.

"There's no such thing," Violet said, but her voice was shaking. She turned and shut the front door, quickly turning the bolt.

A shaft of moonlight was shining through the window and it fell across the carpeted floor. The rest of the house was dark. As Violet and Benny watched, a dark shadow flitted slowly across the moonlit carpet.

"What was that?" asked Benny, grabbing Violet's hand.

"I'm not sure," Violet answered. "Maybe it was a cloud passing in front of the moon."

"But it was shaped like a bat!" Benny cried.

Violet didn't want to frighten Benny, but she knew he was right. A large bat had just slowly passed by the window.

Suddenly the lights flashed on. Henry and Jessie pounded up the basement stairs.

"It was only the switch, just as I thought," Henry said, coming through the door. He stopped in his tracks when he saw the kitchen. Sitting on the table was a glass of milk and a plate with a half-eaten sandwich. Next to them was Benny's library book, *The Legend of the Vampire*, open to page 136.

Violet gasped. "Someone was here!"

"You're right, Violet." Henry walked to the table. "And whoever it was left in a hurry. This glass of milk is still cold."

"And here is the missing key!" Jessie picked up the key from the kitchen counter.

"I think we should go," Violet said.

Henry agreed. "We need to let Mr. Hudson know that someone has been inside his house."

"And it wasn't a vampire," Benny said, nodding at Violet, "because vampires don't eat sandwiches." He picked up his library book and stared at the front cover. "They only like blood!"

"Benny and I heard footsteps outside while you were in the basement," Violet explained. "We need to be very careful."

The children stepped outside and peered

up and down the street. Jessie locked the door tightly and put the key into her pocket. She left the porch light on. The children hurried home as fast as they could.

CHAPTER 9

A Mysterious Photo

Later that night the Aldens sat in the living room each with a mug of hot chocolate and plate of cookies. Henry opened *The Legend of the Vampire* to Chapter One. He began to read.

The cemetery on Whittaker Street was dark and cold. Martha stood by the gate and pulled her coat close around her body. She wrapped her scarf tightly around her neck. A chill ran down her spine, and she turned just in time to see a strange man in a long, dark cape gliding toward her neighbor's quaint little house. At first she had hoped that it was Francis, coming home after all these years. But when she saw the pale, white skin, the blood red lips, and the piercing black eyes of the stranger, she knew that it was not Francis. Those eyes held her for a moment and as they did, Martha felt the blood pounding through her veins. Was it fear or excitement that made her heart flutter so violently? Just as suddenly as he arrived, the stranger disappeared into her neighbor's basement, so quickly that it seemed he simply melted himself through the walls.

"Oh my!" cried Mrs. McGregor standing in the doorway. "What a frightening book to be reading before bed. It would give me nightmares!"

Benny rubbed his eyes and yawned.

"We're looking for clues to a mystery in the story. Strange things are happening at Mr. Hudson's house."

"I've heard about it," Mrs. McGregor said. "Oh yes, and a man named Josh called a few minutes ago. He said Mr. Hudson is coming home tomorrow. It seems he didn't need to stay as long as he'd planned. Also, Josh said you left milk on the table and mud on the porch."

The children looked at each other.

"We'll go over there first thing in the morning." Jessie said.

Henry nodded. "We need to tell Mr. Hudson someone was in his house."

Mrs. McGregor held a bag of mini marshmallows in her hand. "Also, I thought you might like to have some of these in your hot chocolates. Goodnight, children."

They all thanked Mrs. McGregor and wished her a good night.

Jessie reached for the marshmallows and sprinkled a few on the top of her hot chocolate. "Josh must have been at

Mr. Hudson's house tonight."

"But why would he go over there so late?" wondered Violet.

Henry shrugged. "It does seem odd. I doubt he'd to show the house to a buyer late at night."

Benny dropped a few marshmallows into his mug and a whole handful into his mouth. "Maybe he was looking for the vampire."

Henry stood to take a cookie from the platter and *The Legend of the Vampire* fell to the floor. When he picked it up, he saw something sticking out from the pages. It was an old black-and-white photograph. The edges were a little crumpled, and a crease ran down one side.

"Look at this!"

Jessie, Violet, and Benny crowded around the photo in Henry's hand.

"That's Mr. Hudson's house!" Violet pointed to the home that was in the background of the photo.

"Who do you think those two boys are?" asked Benny.

Two young children were posed in front of the porch. One looked to be about Henry's age, fourteen, and the other one seemed to be a little younger than Benny. The younger boy had his hand resting on the seat of a shiny, new bicycle.

Violet gasped. She pointed to the older boy. "That must be Mr. Hudson."

"I'm sure you're right!" Jessie exclaimed. "And the other one must be his little brother."

Benny's fingers were sticky from the marshmallows, so he did not touch the photo. But he pointed at the two boys. "They sure do look an awful lot alike."

"Yes," Violet agreed. "If they were the same age, I would think they were twins."

"But how did the picture get in the book?" Benny wondered. "Do you think it was stuck in that book in the library for all those years?"

Henry turned the photo over in his hand. "No. I don't think it was in the book before today. See this crease mark? I think the photo was folded and carried in someone's wallet for a long time."

Henry pulled his wallet from his back pocket. He slid the picture in and out of the billfold. "See? When it is folded at the crease, this photo fits perfectly in a wallet. You wouldn't need to fold it if you were going to keep it in a book."

"That makes a lot of sense, Henry," Violet said.

"Look, there's some faded writing on the bottom." Jessie took the picture and held it up to the light. "It's hard to read."

Benny ran from the room and quickly returned with a magnifying glass that he had gotten as a gift on his last birthday. "This will help!" he cried.

"Thanks, Benny." Henry held the magnifying glass over the faded writing. It helped the children see the faded ink. Slowly, the Aldens puzzled out each letter.

"'Charles!'" Jessie exclaimed. "The first word is "'Charles!'"

"Mr. Hudson's first name is Charles," Violet remembered.

"A…n…d," Benny read. "'And!' I know that word."

Violet smiled. "Good job, Benny."

The last word was the most faded. Before long, though, the Aldens had spelled "F-r-a-n-c-i-s."

"Francis must be Mr. Hudson's younger brother," Jessie said.

Henry was paging through *The Legend of the Vampire*, checking to see if any more pictures could be stuck between its pages. He did not find any. He paused at the dedication page. "Look at this."

Jessie read aloud: "'This book is dedicated to my dear brother, Francis.'"

"We didn't even have to read the book to find clues in it!" Benny exclaimed.

Henry set the book back on the table with the picture carefully placed inside. "We'll have a lot to tell Mr. Hudson when we see him tomorrow morning."

CHAPTER 10

Caught!

The next morning, after a quick breakfast of cereal and fruit, the Aldens jumped on their bikes and quickly rode to Mr. Hudson's house. But there was a police car in front! It was just driving away as the children walked up the front steps.

Jessie knocked on the front door.

"Come on in, kids," Mr. Hudson called from the living room. He was sitting on the couch, his suitcase dumped on the floor beside the coffee table. His hair was uncombed and there were dark circles under his eyes.

Josh stood in the corner with his hands thrust deeply into his pockets.

"Is everything all right?" Jessie asked. "We just saw the police car."

"The police were here looking for finger-prints," Mr. Hudson said. "Someone has broken into my home!"

Josh stepped forward. "No locks or windows were broken," he said. He stared at the Aldens. "Someone must have left the door unlocked. And it wasn't me!"

Mr. Hudson looked at the children. "I don't blame you," he said. "I even forget to lock the door sometimes. I know you meant well."

"But we *did* lock the door!" Jessie insisted. "We are very responsible. The person who broke into your home knew where the key was hidden. He took it from the shed and let himself in. We found the key last night on the kitchen counter."

Mr. Hudson looked up sharply.

"You must have told some of your friends

where that key was," Josh said accusingly. "Who else could know where the key was hidden?"

"I can promise you that we did not tell anyone," Jessie answered.

Mr. Hudson ran his hands through his hair. "Someone was in the shed," he said. "My plane came in very early this morning. When I got home, I heard noises coming from the shed. I called the police right away. The person in the shed ran away through the cemetery when the police arrived. The officers chased him. I don't know if they caught him yet or not. Perhaps he found the key by accident and let himself in when I was away."

The Aldens looked at each other.

"Was the person who ran from the shed as tall as the vampire that you have been seeing in the cemetery lately?" asked Henry.

"What?" Mr. Hudson sat up very straight. "The vampire? Josh, have you been telling stories?"

"It's not just a story," Josh answered. "You

told me yourself that you saw something strange in the cemetery at night."

"I saw a person," Mr. Hudson explained to the children. "He dressed and acted like the vampire from my book, *The Legend of the Vampire*. Whenever I tried to call out to him or to catch him, he ran away."

"Do you think the person in the shed could have been the one who acted like the vampire?" Henry asked.

"I suppose so," Mr. Hudson answered. "He was about the same height. But who would want to do such a thing? I don't understand."

Jessie put her hand on Mr. Hudson's shoulder. "Mr. Hudson, was there anyone at all besides you who knew where you hid the spare key?"

Mr. Hudson was quiet for some time. "Besides you four children, there might be one other person," he said. "But it couldn't have been him."

The Aldens weren't so sure. "Mr. Hudson," Henry said. "We think it may have been your brother Francis who took the spare key and

let himself into your home."

"Francis? What? How do you know that name?" Mr. Hudson's eyes were wide with surprise.

Benny took the folded photo from the pages of the book and handed it to Mr. Hudson.

Mr. Hudson drew in his breath sharply. He cradled the photo gently in his hands. "Where did you get this?" he finally asked.

"We found it," Benny replied, "stuck between the pages of *The Legend of the Vampire.*"

"This is a picture of my brother and me!" Mr. Hudson cried.

Just then there were heavy footsteps on the front porch. Two police officers opened the screen door and brought in a man in handcuffs. He was dirty and disheveled. He looked almost exactly like Mr. Hudson.

Mr. Hudson jumped to his feet. "Francis!" he cried. He threw his arms around his brother.

The officers looked confused.

"Please, officer," Mr. Hudson asked. "Take those handcuffs off. This has all been a big misunderstanding. This is my brother."

"You're not going to press charges?" asked the officer. "He has already admitted that he broke into your home."

"No, no, of course I'm not going to prosecute," Mr. Hudson said hurriedly. "There has been no crime here. My brother is welcome in this house at any time."

The officer shook his head disapprovingly, but he removed the cuffs. Mr. Hudson thanked the police for all their help and showed them to the door.

After Francis was comfortably seated in a chair with a glass of lemonade and a clean shirt borrowed from his brother, the Aldens explained what they knew.

"While you were away," Henry said, "Benny ran into a man at the library fair who looked exactly like you."

"I thought it was you at first, Mr. Hudson," Benny said. "But then I realized that the man was too..." Benny paused.

"Messy." Francis finished the sentence.

"Yes," Benny agreed, his face coloring. "Mr. Hudson is always dressed so neatly."

"We may look alike," Francis said, "but other than that we are as different as brothers can be."

"We are very different," Mr. Hudson agreed. "And I'm sorry to say that it led to quite a few fights when we were younger."

"I'm sorry about those fights, Charles," Francis said.

"I am, too." Mr. Hudson looked at the Aldens. "Francis and I loved each other, but we disagreed about many things."

"Charles was fussy and neat," Francis said. "His half of the room was always clean and organized. I was a lot a messier and I drove him crazy sometimes."

Mr. Hudson smiled. "And Francis was a great athlete, but I couldn't even run without tripping over my own two feet. Francis liked to go sleep early, especially before big games, while I liked to stay up late reading. He used to be so annoyed with me for keeping the light on."

Both brothers laughed at the memories.

"After our parents died, we fought a lot more often," Francis said.

"I wanted you to stay in school and get a good education," Mr. Hudson remembered.

Francis nodded. "And I wanted to quit school and work in my friend's carpentry shop. One day, after a particularly big fight, I got very angry and I left home without a word. Since then, I've traveled all around the country. I've lived and worked in many different states. My life has been very interesting. But throughout all those years, I always missed my home and my brother."

"Why didn't you call or write?" asked Mr. Hudson. "I always wondered where you were."

"I thought you might not want me back," Francis explained. "I know that I was quite a troublemaker. I was afraid that we would just start fighting again. Then, a few months ago, I finally decided to take the risk and come back and see you. The older I've gotten, the more I've realized how much my family and my old home mean to me. I was going to surprise you. But when I saw the sign on the lawn that said that the house was for sale, I became angry. You weren't ever supposed to sell this house, Charles. Our parents wanted us to keep it in the family as long as we were alive. But I had been gone for so long. I knew I couldn't demand anything from you."

"So you decided to scare away the people who came to buy the house?" Henry asked.

"Yes." Francis hung his head. "I admit it. I pretended to haunt the graveyard at night. I wore a cape and I even sprinkled fake blood on tombstones and people's back porches. I tried to do all the things that the vampire did in the stories you used to tell me when we were growing up. I knew it would start people talking and word would get around. I thought that no one would want to buy a house with a vampire in the backyard."

Henry pulled a small vial from his pocket. "Was this the blood that you used?"

"Yes!" Francis exclaimed. "But it is only

colored water. Where did you find that?"

"You dropped it when we bumped into each other at the library fair," Benny explained. "I tried to catch you to give it back, but you ran away."

"I was worried when you called me 'Mr. Hudson'," Francis said. "I thought you might know who I was. I didn't want Charles to know I was in town until I had finished scaring away all the buyers for the house."

"Did you take *The Legend of the Vampire* from my backpack?" asked Benny.

"I did," Francis said. "I saw you put it in there on that first day that you met my brother. I needed more ideas for my vampire haunting. I knew I could find them in the book."

"And then you left the picture in the book," Jessie added.

"Yes. I was so surprised to see young Benny there at the diner, that I jumped up and left, leaving the book behind. Imagine how surprised I was to find the book on the kitchen table later that night."

"That's because I left it there by accident." Benny sighed.

"I figured as much," Francis said. "The flowers were replanted and the porch was scrubbed. I knew you kids had been here."

"You wrote those terrible words in ink on our front porch?" Charles asked. "How could you do that?"

Francis looked sheepish. "I'm very sorry, Charles. I promise to repaint the porch for you. I was only trying to be a good vampire. But I suppose I didn't do a very good job of it. The Aldens came back to the house at night. I thought they would be too frightened for that."

"We were looking for the book," Benny explained.

"I knew Charles had gone out of town and so I took the key from under the pot. We always kept it there, even when we were children. I was having a nice sandwich and reading by flashlight when you children surprised me. I rushed into the basement. When I heard footsteps on the stairs I had to quickly sneak out the back door. I circled around to the front. I thought I could get back in to get the rest of my sandwich and the book, but these two kids where standing by the door." Francis pointed at Violet and Benny.

"You tried to scare us with a bat," Benny said.

Francis chuckled. He put his two hands together and flapped his fingers as though they were wings. "Remember this, Charles? We used to make all kinds of animal shapes in the shadows at night. I was quite good at it."

"You still are!" Violet said. "It looked very much like a real bat. We were frightened."

Mr. Hudson shook his head. "Francis, I wish you hadn't done all these things. I wish you had just come and talked to me."

Francis sighed. "I know that now. And I'm sorry." Francis turned to Violet. "I apologize for frightening you."

"And where did you put all the 'For Sale' signs that you stole?" asked Mr. Hudson.

"You have to return them to Josh. You upset him as well."

Francis looked confused.

"Your brother didn't steal the 'For Sale' signs," Violet said. "Josh did that."

"What?" Mr. Hudson turned to look at his realtor. "Why would Josh steal his own signs? That doesn't make any sense. He wants to sell the house. It's his job."

Josh stuck his hands even deeper into his pockets. He seemed to be trying to find something to say.

"Josh has a friend who wants your house, Mr. Hudson," Violet explained. "Only he can't afford to buy it unless you lower the price. Josh didn't start the vampire rumors, but he helped them along. He thought that if buyers were frightened away, you would be happy to sell the house for a lot less money to his friend. I saw the missing 'For Sale' signs in the back of Josh's car and I overheard him on the phone with his friend."

Josh's face was bright red. "You should know that it is not right to eavesdrop!" he shouted at Violet.

"I was not eavesdropping!" Violet crossed her arms and stood her ground. "I was working in the garden when you made a call near the front porch. I couldn't help but hear what you said."

"And you should know that you were supposed to be working for me and not for your friend," Mr. Hudson added. "You're fired as my realtor, Josh."

Josh bit hard on his lower lip. He took a few steps toward the door, then turned back around. "I'm very sorry, Charles," he said. "And I'm sorry for accusing you, Violet. My friend doesn't have a lot of money and he has five children. I thought this would be the perfect house for him. But it was wrong of me to try to ruin your chances of selling at a good price. I didn't mean any harm, but I know what I did was wrong. I hope you'll forgive me."

Josh pushed open the screen door to leave just as Mrs. Fairfax was about to knock.

"What is going on over here?" she

complained, stepping into the living room. "All this commotion has got to stop. Realtors, children, police cars. What next?"

"Hello, Martha," said Francis.

"Francis? Is that Francis?" Mrs. Fairfax put her hand over her heart.

Mr. Hudson helped Mrs. Fairfax into a seat. "It's my brother all right, Martha," he said with a smile. "He's come back to live with me."

"So you're not selling the house?" Mrs. Fairfax asked.

Mr. Hudson looked at his brother and paused. "No, I'm not selling. That is," he continued, "as long as Francis agrees to move in and help me out with the house."

Francis stood and threw his arm around his brother's shoulder. "Thank you, Charles," he said. "There is nothing I would like better. It is so good to be home!"

Suddenly, a loud growling noise came from the sofa. Everyone turned to look.

Benny's face turned bright red. He clasped his hands over his stomach. "Excuse me," he apologized.

Everyone laughed, even Mrs. Fairfax.

"I suppose tracking down vampires can make a person quite hungry." Mr. Hudson smiled.

"*Everything* makes Benny hungry," Henry explained.

Mr. Hudson brought out a pitcher of lemonade and set a tray of snacks on the table for his company.

Everyone was excited when Mr. Hudson told them that the producers had agreed to film the movie version of *The Legend of the Vampire*. It was going to be set right in Greenfield.

"Maybe we can all have a role in the film!" Benny cried.

"That would be so exciting," Jessie agreed. "At the very least, perhaps we can come and watch the filming. Would that be all right with you, Mr. Hudson?"

"Of course!" Mr. Hudson said. "You are more than welcome."

"Are you going to write any more books,

Mr. Hudson?" Violet asked.

"I never stop writing, Violet," Mr. Hudson said. "And I'm always looking for ideas for my next story."

As Benny reached for a third helping of cheese and crackers, his stomach let out another loud growl.

Mr. Hudson laughed. "Maybe my next book could be called *The Legend of the Bottomless Stomach*."

"And if that book is made into a movie, I could have the lead role!" Benny grinned. "I knew my stomach would make me famous!"